THE JUDAS CREW

Trevor Preston

THE JUDAS CREW

NO EXIT PRESS

First published 2000 by No Exit Press,
18 Coleswood Road, Harpenden, Herts, AL5 1EQ

www.noexit.co.uk

A CIP catalogue record for this book is available
from the British Library

ISBN 1–901982–78–5 The Judas Crew

2 4 6 8 10 9 7 5 3 1

Typeset by Palimpsest Book Production Limited,
Polmont, Stirlingshire
Printed and bound in Great Britain by
Cox and Wyman, Reading, Berkshire

For my father Bob Preston

Prologue

A day of wind and rain had left behind a wild spiky night, bright moonlight gave everything a hard brittle edge. Beyond the barren marshlands stranded pools of light hung over a motorway that led to the city.

Powerful spotlights pricked the darkness, the roar of engines invaded the silence. A posse of expensive off-roaders, their bodies scabbed with mud, drove across the desolate landscape. They slowed and gathered, dogs barked. There was a brawl of drunken voices: these were men of the city at odds with anything approaching nature.

One of the men got out and lifted a box from the back of his vehicle. He stepped into the darkness beyond the arc of lights, placed the box on the ground and opened it. A fox emerged, suspiciously sniffing the sharp night air, then sensing freedom it darted into the darkness. The waiting lampers, with howls of drunken delight, released their dogs and went hunting city style.

The fox ran for its life, darting and weaving, trying to escape the probing beams. The vehicles, their engines screaming, wheels churning plumes of dirt, powered over the wilderness. In a blood frenzy the lampers urged the dogs on for a kill. One of them was using a video camera to record the full horror of their sport.

Trapped in a net of lights, the fox began to tire as the dogs ran it down. Then in one sickening moment they were on it, teeth white blades, ripping it to pieces in the harsh tungsten lights.

The cameraman scrambled from his vehicle and ran to get as close as he could to record the kill. The other sportsmen had left their vehicles, to witness the death of the fox. One of them snatched what was left from the dogs while the rest formed themselves into a group for the camera. The man carried the bloody carcass back to the group and took his place. He held the fox up by the scruff of its neck, its dead eyes reflecting the lights.

A cold wind knifed the air as the lampers returned to their vehicles and drove slowly back into the darkness, leaving behind them a new sort of silence.

One

At night in the city the zoo is on the streets: dossers foraging restaurant dustbins, young toms with habits giving punters head in parked cars, boosters looking for stolen-to-order steel, junkies with cardboard eyes searching for jellies and smack, kids on the skids doing crack on bent Coca Cola cans, cannibals wearing cargo burning to be somebody, thieves, con men, touts, drifters, winos, dips, scufflers, strippers moving from venue to venue, rogue cabbies running whores to hotels, the chicken man checking his coop of rent boys, punks into petty villainy, the real bad guys going to work – the law looking to step on them. In the darkest hours you can smell the sweetness of hell.

In one of the marginal parts of the city where lives are lived that are scarcely bearable, a man ran for his life pursued by three cars. He ran as though trying to separate himself from his fear. At the end of each section of derelict houses the cars cut him off and fixed him with their lights, toying with him, an insect in a downturned glass.

He paused for a few stalled seconds, his chest heaving, trying to pump some oxygen back into his burning lungs, then he was on the move again; all that kept him going was the certainty that if he stopped he was lost.

The cars closed in, the game was over.

Pinned by lights to a wall, the human fox waited for his tormentors to make their move.

Seaman and Connell stepped from one of the cars and approached. They stood facing him, without speaking. Seaman had piercing driftless blue eyes and a stave of music tattooed on the side of his neck. Connell was built like a barn, the slabs of flesh of his weight-trained body straining at the leather of his jacket.

Joey Pyke, his chest still heaving, stabs of breath smoking from his mouth into the cold night air, raised his hands in a conciliatory gesture and made a last desperate effort at an appeal for reason. 'Look . . . look . . . listen . . .' He had a sallow face and eyes that never seemed to settle. 'Listen . . .'

Seaman lit a cigarette and exhaled a scarf of smoke. 'I'm listening.'

'You got it all wrong.'

'Really?'

'You and Pauli.'

'Is that right?'

'They done me to fuck, Dave!'

'Who?'

'I don't know.'

'You don't know?'

'It was all done on the phone.'

'No names?'

'I swear to Christ!'

'You're taking the risk, they're taking the long money, and you don't even ask their names?'

'I know what it sounds like.'

'Where's the case?'

'It sounds fuckin' ridiculous.'

'Where's the case, Joey?'

'I don't know.'

'You wanna shit blood?'

'I don't know. If I did I'd tell you!'

'Who's got it?'

'They have.'

'Who?'

Pyke's desperation turned to anger. 'I don't fuckin' know! I keep tellin' you!'

'What was it, Joey, a little "Fuck you!" to Pauli?'

'Why would I do that?'

Seaman shrugged. 'Why would you?'

'I wouldn't do that.'

'Pauli treated you right?'

'Yeah.'

'Decent?'

'He did.'

'Didn't he? Always?'

'Pauli's good stuff.'

'And you do this to him you horrible little fucker!' Pyke was stiff with fear. 'Frankie Pitillo told me that . . .'

Seaman cut him off. 'I've talked to Frankie.'

'He told me Pauli was outa the frame.'

'Frankie said that?'

'He did!'

Seaman shook his head. 'Frankie never said that.'

'He told me Pauli had pulled out of the deal, that he was layin' down some moves on something else. Then I get a call from these people. They offer me ten large to front it up for them . . .'

Seaman stepped forward and stabbed his cigarette out on Pyke's face.

Pyke's cry of pain was stifled as Connell grabbed and held him. Seaman pulled a polythene bag from a pocket, slipped it over Pyke's head and twisted it tight. Pyke fought for breath like a fish out of water, his head twisting, the bag misting. When Seaman pulled the bag off Pyke gulped down great lungfuls of air.

Seaman leaned into him. 'Now, lie to me again Joey and you're goin' down a fuckin' hole!'

Pyke sucked in gasps of air.

'Where's the case?'

Pyke just managed to talk. 'Pocket . . . ticket.'

Seaman searched his pockets and found a left-luggage ticket. He looked back at Pyke. 'It better be there.' He took out his wallet and placed the ticket carefully into one of the credit card slots.

'Why? Why did you do it, Joey?'

Pyke started to laugh.

It took Seaman by surprise. 'Funny?'

Pyke didn't care any more. He'd passed that point where fear becomes so overwhelming it becomes fatuous.

Seaman stiffened. 'You think it's funny?'

Pyke took out a crumpled pack of cigarettes, still laughing. He slipped one between his dry lips. 'You're right. It was a "Fuck you!" to Pauli. I fuckin' hate the cunt! Always have. I don't know no one who likes him. He's a fucking disease!'

Seaman slapped the cigarette out of Pyke's mouth, his anger spilling over. 'You're not worth a fuckin' rub, are you?' He slipped a gun from inside his coat and shot Pyke in both arms.

Pyke dropped to the pavement, the pain so great it silenced him. Blood poured down his jacket sleeves and formed into pools.

Connell and Seaman made their way back to the

waiting vehicles. As the cars dissolved into the darkness a stray dog appeared, its ribs like knives in a box. It cautiously approached the crippled man, sniffing at him, then started to lick the fresh blood from the pavement.

The squash club bar looked like a bar on a luxury liner: lots of expensive wood veneer, polished brass trims and an ocean-green carpet. There were buttoned imitation-leather chairs, tables made from antique ships wheels with plate-glass tops, several large aquariums of tropical fish were set into the walls. On a good night, if you were well flavoured, you would swear you could feel the ship rolling.

The members were an odd mix: squash freaks thin as compass needles sipping fizzy water, body builders who used the gym posing at the bar, minor villains wearing sovereign rings whacking back double vodkas, young south London businessmen with their fascist dreams and mobile phones, and a gaggle of women with scratchy voices dressed in shopping mall haute couture with too much make-up, smoking like diesels.

Pauli West sat in his office drinking tea and playing a game of patience. A small CCT monitor on his desk kept him in touch with what was happening in the club. He was a man who had no gift for intimacy: no one got close to him, he trusted no one completely, and he showed no mercy to those too disposed to trust; they were his natural prey. His was a rounded closed world, a sub culture totally opposed to the basic idea of justice and order. Pauli West was a criminal's criminal who thrived in the moral squalor of a city that glowed with greed.

He scooped up the cards and started to lay them

out again. He had a dangerous elegance: his fine-boned hands were too fragile, too calm, not the hands of someone who'd beaten a man to death with his own shoe.

The office door opened and Seaman entered.

West's eyes never left the cards.

Seaman took out his wallet. 'Left luggage.' He slipped the ticket out. 'Euston.'

West got up from the desk and crossed to a drinks cabinet. 'Any trouble?'

Seaman placed the ticket on the desk and smiled. 'Not for us.'

West opened the cabinet, took out a bottle of good whisky and two glasses. 'What happened?'

'I clipped his wings.'

West put the glasses on the desk and poured two drinks. He handed one to Seaman. 'What I'd like to know is, who squared him up?'

Seaman sipped his drink. 'He says he don't know. It was all done by phone.'

West picked the ticket up and looked at it. 'He's lying! It was someone close, it had to be. Someone we know.'

'Nicky Mobbs?'

West sipped his whisky. 'Nicky didn't know about it.'

Seaman finished his drink. 'It's fuckin' funny that Nicky goes missin' just before this goes off.'

West held the ticket out to Seaman. 'Pick it up in the morning.'

Seaman took the ticket. 'Where do I take it?'

West settled behind his desk again. 'Get it to Frankie. I'll give him a call.'

Seaman turned to leave. 'Is Monday night still on?'

West picked up the cards. 'Monday?'

'That new club. We're taking Fran.'

West started to lay the cards out again. 'That's right.'

Seaman glanced at West lost in the logic of the cards and left the office, closing the door quietly.

Outside the rail terminus the autumn sky was unrelenting blue, inside the same sky, pressed against the diesel-stained Perspex roof, was the colour of washed-out overalls. The morning rush had subsided; most of the tracks stood empty, a crane of diesel smoke rose from a locomotive as its engine warmed up with a throbbing rattling roar.

Seaman entered the terminus and made his way directly to the left-luggage booth. He presented the ticket to a young guy with an ascetic pale face and long hair who looked like something left over from the Last Supper.

He disappeared into the back and soon returned carrying an expensive silver metal business case with combination locks. Seaman paid the charge, then with a quick glance around to make sure he wasn't being watched, he carried the case out of the station to a car waiting in the forecourt taxi area and got into the back.

Connell was driving. He accelerated away and slipped the car into the stream of traffic on the busy road outside.

Seaman had the case on the back seat and was checking the locks. He looked up at Connell. 'Got that screwdriver?'

Connell reached under his seat, lifted up a screwdriver and passed it over his shoulder to Seaman.

Seaman levered the locks open and lifted the lid.

The business case was neatly packed with quarter kilos of cocaine. Seaman took a penknife from his pocket, opened the blade and made a small incision in one of the packets. He pinched out a snort of cocaine and tested it, rubbing what was left on his fingers into his gums. He could see Connell watching him in the rear view mirror. He looked up and smiled. 'I reckon we've earned a little taste.' He took a small silver snuff box from a pocket and packed it with coke.

Frankie Pitillo was rail thin with the ghost face of a heavy user. One ear had a lobe missing; it had been bitten off in a fight. He was a slippery bastard — trying to get hold of Frankie was like trying to find an eel's arse.

Frankie looked the case over, saw the cut bag and the missing coke, and looked at Seaman. 'Pauli said to give you a bag. Better be this one, eh?'

Seaman was well pleased. 'What'll that fetch on the street, Frankie?'

'Tell you what.' Frankie nodded across the room at Connell. 'You and Terry take what you want for personal use, and I'll sell what's left for a flat monkey commission.'

When they were gone Frankie transferred the cocaine to a rusting metal toolbox and took it out to his car. He drove across London and out into the bleak Essex countryside to an isolated roadside garage that was all but derelict. The old pumps had been vandalised, the windows were boarded up, the door to the main building was chained and padlocked.

Frankie let himself in.

He'd grown used to the cloying stink of decay and sump oil. There were fans of cobwebs and ribbons of dust everywhere. An old Humber Super Snipe had been left stranded over a working pit, its dust-encrusted engine still hung from a heavy block and tackle over the front of the once luxury car. Frankie hid the tool box under a pile of oily rags with a verdigris mould growing on them.

On his way back to London his mobile rang. He picked it up and switched it on.

'Yeah?'

'We're going to need someone for the Essex run.'

'I've got someone in mind.'

'Do I know him?'

'No, but he's smart and he's useful.'

'Line him up.'

'I'm seeing him Monday.'

'That's leaving it a bit tight.'

'It's gonna be okay, Pauli, I promise you. He's tasty.'

'Keep in touch.'

'Yeah.'

Two

John Mahon drove through the city. He was a tall spare man, a quiet man who never used two words where one would do. He occupied space in a dangerous way. There was something deeply secret about Mahon, it was in his eyes; he was a man who had drawn a veil between himself and his past. Brought up on the west coast of Ireland, he was exiled here. He felt uneasy in the city; he knew there were things you couldn't see or touch but they were there. He cut through the backstreets, occasionally glancing out to check the night people. A tape of Willie Nelson's 'Spirit' played softly. Mahon was on a slow trawl, supplying his people with wraps of lady and scag. They trusted him; he sold them good shit at a fair price and he was cautious.

The car emerged from a dark side street into the bright cave of clubland and joined the shoal of slow-moving traffic, the drivers' faces reflected like ghosts in the windscreens. Although it was late autumn and the weather had turned cold, there was still a scatter of tourists lost in the maze of shivering streets.

*   *   *

A huge spade in a black coat was minding the door of an exclusive club where those still feeding off the carcass of Thatcher came to play. A chauffeur-driven Bentley pulled up and one of the unpleasantly rich and his girlfriend got out. They walked to the entrance as the Bentley hissed away. The rich dick was a regular. He greeted the doorman in a patronising voice he reserved for serviles. 'Good evening, Harold.'

Harold loathed these people but he didn't give a sweet tomorrow; he could play their game as long as the tips kept coming. 'Good evening, sir.' He towered over them. The woman took in his size with wonderment. He nodded politely to her. His voice was rich and dark. 'Madam.'

'Good evening.' She was fascinated. 'Harold?'

'Yes, madam, Harold.'

'How tall are you?'

'Six ten, madam.'

Her voice filled with amazement. 'Six feet ten inches?'

'Yes, madam.' He went to reach past the woman. 'Excuse me.' He deliberately brushed her body with his arm as he opened the door of the club. As they stepped through into the foyer he heard the woman, still amazed. 'The size of him!'

Harold smiled. He knew he was into a tidy little tip from that one. He could always tell; she was probably laying bets with herself right now on the size he was south of the belt buckle.

As he closed the door he saw a Lexus pull up. Seaman was driving, on his nightly tour to check the venues that his outfit 'Seaman Securities' were employed to protect.

The driver's window whined down and Seaman looked out at him.

Harold left the door and moved down to the car. He bent his massive bulk to talk to Seaman. 'You're late.'

'Yeah, well behind.' The clothes and the car were well-heeled west London, but Dave Seaman was and always would be a Bermondsey boy.

Harold sensed he was not happy. 'Had a problem?'

'You could call it that.'

'Who with?'

'Some wheel in one of the clubs.'

'What about?'

'He said Arnie had been dipping the bar till.'

'Is that right?'

'Arnie said he didn't.'

Harold smiled. 'That's original.'

'That's not the point,' snapped Seaman.

Harold wondered what the point was.

'He started to threaten him with some hot shot ex-boxer from the kitchens.'

Harold picked up on this. 'Billy Auld.'

'What?'

'That has to be Billy Auld.'

'Who?'

'Very useful heavyweight in his day.' Harold was a big fight fan, he knew all about the old boxers. 'He works there as a chef.'

Seaman dismissed it. 'Anyway, it's sorted.'

Harold had to smile. 'He'd have sorted Arnie if it had come to it.'

Seaman was already on to his next venue. 'Well it didn't, did it?' he said sharply.

'He could bang a bit, that boy,' Harold said, determined to have the last word.

Seaman changed the subject. He nodded at the night club. 'Everything all right here?'

This was a soft job. Harold liked it here. 'Sweet.'

Seaman pressed the button to raise the window. 'Lovely, lovely, that's how it should be.'

Harold drew back as the window whined up and watched the car seep back into the night traffic.

Stumpy Redman, an old black jazzer, his grey moustache kippered with nicotine, was slumped in a chair in the shabby band room of one of those basement clubs where the liquor is watered and the women for sale. There was a world weariness about the old man; nothing surprised him any more. The way he had lived his life he should have been dead years ago.

A knock at the door alarmed Stumpy. He looked up and called out in broad Brooklyn, 'Aint nobody here.'

The door opened and Mahon entered.

Stumpy was pleased to see him. 'How ya doin', Irish?'

The band room was freezing. Mahon closed the door. 'Christ it's cold in here.'

Stumpy stayed in his chair. 'Cold enough to hang meat.'

Mahon moved towards him. 'Have you said something?'

Stumpy shrugged. 'What's the point?'

'You've got to tell them,' Mahon insisted.

Stumpy looked defeated. 'They won't take no notice of a broken down old schlep like me.'

Mahon took in Stumpy's condition. He looked exhausted and ill. 'Have you eaten?'

Stumpy wheezed a nicotine laugh. 'Lobster and a fine Chablis.'

Mahon stood looking down at the old man. He was a sack of bones. 'You've got to eat.'

Stumpy turned to his saxophone case propped against a wall. 'Wanna drink?'

'I said eat!'

Stumpy opened the case. 'Eat, drink, same fuckin' thing.' Inside was a near-empty bottle of cheap brandy and a chipped glass. 'Born, work, dream, die; life is mostly wastin' time.' He raised the bottle to a bare light bulb to check the level. 'We come into this world good and we go out bad.'

Mahon took in the old man's weary fatalism.

There wasn't much brandy left. Stumpy looked up at Mahon and smiled. 'Fuckin' mice have been at this.' Stumpy would never change; it was too late. He'd spent most of his seventy-odd years laughing at life.

Mahon took out a gram wrap of smoking heroin and palmed it to the old man.

Stumpy dropped the wrap in a pocket and took out a fold of notes. He passed the money to Mahon who pocketed it uncounted. The old man had grown used to the dealer's brief visits. His thumb of a face creased into a lopsided grin. 'I've been talkin' to the fuckin' walls all night.' He unscrewed the cap on the bottle of brandy, half filled the glass and held it out to Mahon. 'Stay and talk.'

Mahon looked at the lonely old man. They both knew that the business of knowing someone took time. It was mysterious; at a push neither of them really wanted to make the effort.

'Sorry, Stumpy, I can't.'

The old man fell back into his posture of defeat and turned to one of the windows. 'Funny things.'

Mahon was lost. 'What?'

'Windows.' The old man raised the glass to his lips. 'Dontcha think?'

Mahon suspected he was being hooked into a conversation.

Stumpy threw the brandy down his throat. 'I read once that if you're inside looking out, a window means hope,' he poured himself another drink and downed it with the same deft movement, 'but if you're outside looking in, you're fucked.'

Mahon turned to the window; all he could see through the grime was a cliff of decaying bricks. He turned back to the old man. 'I've got to go, Stumpy.'

'I've been outside looking in all my life,' Stumpy continued, ignoring Mahon's glance at the door. 'Reckon I was born under a ladder,' the old man was into his history, 'working for chump-change in sties like this.' He cast his eyes mournfully round the shabby room.

Mahon knew that he'd never get away once Stumpy got started. He appealed to him. 'I've got stuff to do, people to see, Stumpy.'

But the old man was intent on holding Mahon as long as he could. 'Did I ever tell you about the time I was with Ike Quebec?' The years had congealed into decades for Stumpy. 'When was it? Fifties? Sixties?'

Mahon started to drift towards the door. 'I'll be by tomorrow.'

'Fuck it! Can't remember nothin' nowadays!'

At the door Mahon turned back sympathetically to Stumpy. 'Maybe we can talk then.'

Stumpy knew he couldn't hold him any longer. 'Be good to yourself, Irish. You take care. There's a lot of very violent people out there.'

Mahon opened the door and turned back to Stumpy with a look of resignation. 'Life goes on.'

Stumpy raised his bony shoulders and spread his hands in a junkie's shrug. 'Only if you let it.'

Mahon watched the old man empty the last of the brandy into the glass. It spilled over the top and dripped onto his lap. He sipped the top off then looked at Mahon hovering by the open door. 'Try to catch the late set.'

Mahon knew the old man was talking about the only thing he really cared about, the only thing he loved, jazz.

Stumpy closed his eyes, his smile was beatific. 'Sweet sounds.' He looked back to the door but Mahon was gone. He finished the brandy, lifted the gram wrap from his pocket and looked at it – an old friend.

Away from the bleak glamour of clubland, Mahon was on the move again, heading through Chelsea. Willie Nelson oozed from the radio. He turned off the Kings Road into a quiet residential square and parked.

He got out and walked with a slow easy stride down one side of the square. As he turned the corner he saw a Porsche parked in the shadows. By instinct he checked briefly around then moved down to the waiting car and got in.

Miles Hollander, prematurely balding, mollusc eyes, turned to Mahon. 'You're late.' He made a point of peevishly checking his watch to emphasise the dealer's lateness. 'I thought you weren't coming.'

Hollander had always irritated Mahon, but he ignored him and lifted a small pinch-seal polythene bag from his pocket. 'A quarter, right?' He passed the bag to him.

Hollander slipped a cheque from a pocket and offered it to Mahon.

Mahon fixed him with a look.

Hollander knew that he had crossed the line. 'I didn't have time to go to the bank.'

Mahon grabbed Hollander's wrist in a powerful grip, his voice tightened. 'I thought we understood each other.' He forced his hand open and took the quarter of cocaine back.

Hollander panicked. 'I can get it for you in the morning.'

Mahon dropped the bag back in his pocket then turned and opened the door. 'You're boring me.'

As he went to get out of the car Hollander reached out and grabbed his shoulder.

Mahon stiffened; he did not like to be touched.

Realising what he was doing, Hollander quickly removed his hand. 'I've got enough cash for a gram.'

Mahon considered.

'Please.' There was a hint of desperation in Hollander's voice.

Mahon closed the door.

'Please,' Hollander begged. 'I wasn't thinking. I'm sorry.'

Mahon turned to him but said nothing.

Hollander pulled screwed up notes from a pocket and nervously started to smooth them. 'I'll go to the bank first thing.'

Mahon took the money, lifted a gram wrap of cocaine from a pocket and held it out to Hollander. 'Don't bother.'

Hollander took the coke. He was confused. 'What do you mean?'

Mahon looked at Hollander then his eyes slid past him into the darkness. 'I don't like you.' He opened the door. 'Never have.'

Mahon got out of the car and walked slowly back

round the square. Hollander was a memory he'd rather
not have.

Mahon's car was parked in a narrow side street carved
with shadows. He had his head back against the seat
rest, his eyes closed. The muzzle of a gun came in
through the open window and pressed into his temple.
His eyes snapped open, his body tensed, and then
with alarming speed he snatched his head to one
side, gripped the gun hand and wrenched it forward.
The gunman's arm was pulled into the car, his body
rammed up against the vehicle.

'It's me!'

Mahon recognised the voice. 'Sweets?' He turned
and saw Sweets welded to the side of the car.

'It's a replica!'

Mahon snatched the replica gun from Sweets and
hurled it out of the window. It clattered down the
pavement.

Sweets went and picked it up then came back to the
car. 'Can I have my arm back?'

'I could've hurt you.'

Sweets measured his arms against each other, one
was a hand longer. 'No good for wallpapering now.'
He laughed and got in the car beside Mahon. Sweets
was a small man; if he had been two inches shorter he
could have joined a circus. His eyesight was poor; his
iguana eyes were guarded by bottle bottom glasses. He
was Mahon's only friend, the only man he trusted. He
was also his eyes and ears. Sweets knew everyone,
he knew where the bodies were buried, and he knew
the rules.

He looked at Mahon. 'You okay?'

'Yeah – why?'

'You was asleep.'

'Just resting.' Mahon checked his watch. 'I'm waiting to see someone.'

'Left your window open.'

'Yeah.'

'Not round here you don't. They piss in your ear for fun then they cut your throat and rob you blind!'

'What are you doing here?'

Sweets pointed up the street. 'Old china of mine, we shared a peter in Gartree.'

Mahon knew that Sweets never went anywhere without good reason. 'Business or pleasure?'

'Bit of both.' Sweets grinned. 'Billy's into computers.' The grin broadened. 'Literally.'

His good humour was catching; when Sweets was around Mahon couldn't help seeing everything as a huge joke. 'What are you up to you little rat?'

Ever since the police had used a lip reader in a club where Sweets was having a meet with certain associates, he had never lost the habit of putting his hand over his mouth when he talked naughties. 'Ever heard of sym theft?'

Mahon nodded. 'Yes.'

Sweets was surprised. 'You have?'

'Micro chips.'

'It's a doddle.'

Mahon didn't want to down Sweets but he thought he ought to know. 'You're too late.'

'What do you mean too late?'

'It's all changed.'

'What?'

'All over.'

'What do you mean?'

Mahon tried to explain as simply as he could. 'A chip worth fifty pounds a couple of years ago is worth fifty pence now.'

'Fifty pence?'

'Yes.'

'Bullshit!'

'Don't you read the papers? The companies that make micro chips are going bust, they're closing their plants down.' Nothing usually fazed this little man but Sweets looked a touch crestfallen. 'Anyway,' Mahon continued, 'you're a grifter, Sweets. When was the last time you broke in anywhere?'

'Offices? Easy.'

'You think so?'

'Walk in, do the biz, walk out.'

'Not with hundreds of thousands of pounds of heavy-duty hardware in them they're not.'

'Billy reckons that half the alarm systems don't even work.'

'Yeah, but which half?'

'He's been at it since he was thirteen.'

'How old is he now?'

'About my age. Why?'

'How much time has he done?'

The question took Sweets by surprise. 'What?'

'Simple question.'

'Fair bit I suppose.'

'How much?'

Sweets shrugged. 'I dunno.'

'A decent guess?'

'Bits and pieces.'

'What was his last lot?'

'A seven.'

'So – what? Twelve?'

Sweets nodded. 'Twelve, twelve plus.'

'How much have you done?'

'Not counting remand?'

'Tariff?'

'Altogether?'

'You did a two at Gartree . . .'

'And I got a five which was reduced to time served on appeal.'

'Sixteen months?'

'That's right. And twelve months for receiving.'

'Less than five years? He's either very unlucky or not very smart. I'd stick to grifting if I were you, Sweets.'

Sweets suddenly stiffened. 'Let's get out of here!'

Mahon started the car and drove off. He knew better than to question Sweets; he had an instinct for trouble that was uncanny.

Sweets glanced briefly back.

Mahon turned to him. 'What was it?'

'See the car?'

Mahon had seen a car pull into the street.

Sweets removed his glasses. 'I know that car. Filth from Vine Street.'

Mahon knew this probably meant one thing. 'Billy?'

Sweets polished the lenses of his glasses on his shirt collar. 'He's either a grass or they're round to give him a tug.'

Mahon looked at him. 'Nice timing, Sweets.'

Sweets was irrepressible. He put his glasses back on and grinned. 'You can't be optimistic with a misty optic.'

Three

Jimmy Ryan, little but lethal, south London's answer to Joe Pesci, was with a good-looking sixties soul spade called J.W. They sat at a table in the squash club bar that looked down into an empty court; light fizzed off the white walls and varnished floor.

Tonight was karaoke night. The club was crowded and noisy, there was a crush of people at the bar. A sound system blared and a large screen showed a selection of fuzzy pop videos. Punters got up on a small stage to do their party piece. Most of them were embarrassing but they didn't give a toss; this was their three minutes of stardom once a week.

Ryan turned to the bar. 'Where's our drinks then?'

J.W. turned and saw Pete Soge giving some good-looking sort at the bar the treatment. 'Who's the mystery with Pete?'

Ryan thought he recognised her. 'She's "Job".'

J.W. didn't know if he was serious. 'You what?'

Ryan looked her over again; now he was sure. 'Detective Constable.'

'Are you serious?' J.W. asked.

'Did the paperwork on me once.'

J.W. was unsettled. 'Stop it, Jimmy.'

Ryan was serious. 'I'm tellin' yer, she's "Job".'

J.W. was alarmed. He took another look. 'Does Pete know?'

Ryan lit a cigarette, he seemed unconcerned. 'Probably.'

J.W. watched them trying to read the situation. 'Look at her, she's all over him.'

Ryan took another look. 'You know Pete: as long as they've got two tits, a hole and a heartbeat.'

J.W. was a worrier. 'What's she doin' here?'

Nothing worried Jimmy. 'Maybe she's a member?'

J.W. was sceptical. 'Yeah, and maybe she isn't. Maybe she's got her nose up us.'

Ryan turned back and studied them; Soge was irritatingly good-looking, the woman was obviously enjoying his attention. Ryan turned and smiled at J.W. 'She don't look like she's workin'.'

J.W. saw Soge detach himself from the woman and head back to the table. He was relieved. 'Here he comes.'

'Don't say nothin',' Ryan whispered as he watched Soge push his way through the hedge of people. 'Let me.' Soge made his way back to the table with a James Caan walk. Ryan saw that he was empty-handed. 'Where's the drinks then?'

Soge nodded back to the bar. 'She's gonna bring 'em over.'

'Who?' asked J.W. sharply, thinking he meant the mystery.

Soge grinned. 'The new barmaid.' He settled back at the table. 'She's a toots.'

'Which one?' J.W. asked.

Soge pointed her out. 'The tidy little blonde.'

She was tidy enough in a fluffy way, smiled a lot, good teeth.

J.W. turned back to Soge. 'She's not new.'

Soge took another look at her. She was talking to one of the other barmaids, explaining something. 'You sure?'

J.W. glanced at her again. 'I've seen her before.'

The barmaid was talking with her hands in tiny gestures, the index fingers and thumbs were pinched as though she was milking a mouse.

Ryan checked her out. 'Looks like a fuckin' poodle, all that hair.'

Soge knew Jimmy was trying to needle him. 'You behave.'

Ryan grinned. 'I had a bird once with a poodle, had this diamante collar and lead. I said to her that must've cost, she said it did, I said it still looks like a fuckin' rat on a rope.'

J.W. turned to Ryan. 'She reminds me of that little stripper you pulled.'

Ryan was not having this. 'Fuck off, she was gorgeous.'

J.W. turned to Soge and winked. 'The ugly ones he blanks.'

Soge patted his pockets for his lighter. 'He don't understand: they're the ones that stick it to you.'

J.W. took out a cheap plastic lighter; the six inch flame that came from it nearly burned the end of Soge's nose.

Soge snatched his head back. 'You takin' a course in welding!'

J.W. looked at the lighter. 'Six fer a pound – rubbish!' He tossed it down into the empty court; it landed with a clatter on the wooden floor.

Soge found his Zippo and lit his cigarette. He turned to Ryan and picked up on the stripper. 'You took her to my flat.'

Ryan looked at him. 'Who?'

'That little sheeny stripper, remember?'

Ryan corrected him. 'She was an exotic dancer.'

Soge ignored this. 'At my place, remember?'

'No.'

'Yes yer do.'

'Remind me.'

'You was upstairs with her in my bed, on that hidden camera I had. She never knew. Me an' J was downstairs watchin' you on the telly.'

Ryan continued to gee him. 'I don't remember that.' He turned to J.W. 'Do you J?'

J.W. was a master of the put on. He turned to Soge. 'When was this then, Pete?'

Soge was taken in. 'Just before Christmas.' Ryan and J.W. looked at each other and shrugged. Soge couldn't believe it; they must remember something that sordid. He turned to J.W. 'We watched 'em rumpin'.'

'Rumpin'?' Ryan turned to J.W. with a look of feigned innocence. 'What does he mean J?'

J.W. looked serious. 'I think it means having carnal knowledge of.' He turned to Ryan. 'It's biblical.'

Ryan looked back at Soge disgusted.

Soge turned to J.W. for confirmation. 'She was a turn, don't you remember J? You said so.'

'I did?'

'She was a goer – bum goin' like a bee's wing.'

The woman Soge had been talking to stood watching them from the bar. Ryan flicked a glance at her then looked at Soge. 'Know who she is?'

'Who?'

Ryan pointed. 'The one you was talkin' to?'

'Yeah.'

'Who?'

'Works in a bettin' shop.'

'That what she told yer?'

'She does,' Soge insisted.

Ryan looked away. 'You lump.'

Soge was lost. 'What are you on about?'

J.W. turned to Ryan. 'Look at her looking.'

Soge was mystified. 'What is all this?'

Ryan turned back to him. 'She's "Job".'

Soge laughed. 'Fuck off!'

'Detective Constable.'

Soge could see that they weren't pissing around now; they really did believe this. 'I've known her fer years.'

Ryan did a double take. 'What?'

'Went out with her.'

Ryan wanted this right. 'You sure?'

'Joey Stebbins' sister.'

Ryan was amazed. 'That's Angie Stebbins? We used ter poke grass up her fanny when we was kids.'

J.W. looked accusingly at Ryan.

Soge was starting to enjoy this. He panned a look between them. 'You two got a shake on over Angie Stebbins?'

A big man with work-thickened hands and a face as blank as a cabbage got up on the stage and started squeezing out 'My Way' on the karaoke mike.

The fluffy barmaid came over to them carrying a tray with three large scotches on it. She smiled nervously; there was lipstick on her teeth. 'Sorry it took so long.' She lowered the tray and started placing the drinks in front of them. 'We've bin ever so busy.'

Ryan had seen Pauli West enter the bar. He turned to the barmaid. 'Buzz off.'

She looked at Ryan. 'Sorry?'

He picked up the tray and slapped it back in her hands. 'Get lost!' She moved away glancing back, offended.

Soge was not pleased. 'What the fuck did you do that for, Jimmy?'

Ryan indicated with the merest movement of his head. 'Here comes the colonel.'

Pauli West was one of those men who through sheer presence appeared bigger than he was. As he crossed the bar the crush of people parted like the Red Sea. People greeted him, but it was fear masquerading as respect. He pulled out a chair and sat at the table.

J.W. turned to him. 'I thought you were taking Fran out.'

West took out a cigarette, tapped and fired it. 'Dave's collecting her after he's finished his rounds.'

'Now that is a good-looking woman,' Ryan observed, looking at Soge. 'I could use some of that.'

West looked at Ryan, his eyes as hard and cold as stones.

Ryan knew from the look that he was out of order; he was talking about Ray Tolman's wife. Ray was doing fifteen on the Moor for importing heroin, but he had an appeal in; he could be out in three months, back on the street. Tolman was frighteningly violent; twice he'd been sent up for murder, twice he'd got off by sending West to intimidate witnesses. Ray Tolman and Pauli West went back a long way, they had grown up together, they were as close as fingers.

Ryan tried to square it with West. 'No offence.'

Pauli made a point of picking up Ryan's scotch and drinking it. 'You should watch that mouth of yours, Jimmy.'

J.W. tactfully got between them. 'When's Ray's new trial?'

West turned from Ryan. 'We don't know yet.'

'Fifteen in the Stone Hotel is a lot of years; that place can break a man,' Soge said philosophically.

West didn't want to discuss it. He moved on to other business. 'What's the latest on Nicky Mobbs?'

Soge looked at him. 'Nothin'.'

West turned to him. 'Say that again?'

Soge looked uneasy. 'He's away, Pauli.'

'Where?'

'No one knows,' said Soge, flicking ash on the floor. 'No one's seen the bastard.'

J.W. sipped his drink. 'He knows it's on him.'

West panned a glance round the group. 'He must be somewhere.'

Ryan tried to get back in. 'It's a fuckin' mystery, Pauli.'

West stabbed out his cigarette. 'You're not trying.'

Soge protested. 'Ah, cummon, Pauli.'

West flared. 'Find him!'

'Where you takin' Fran tonight?' J.W. asked, trying to calm things. West looked at him but didn't answer. 'In case we need to find you.'

West got up to leave. 'That new club, the American one.'

'Who's doin' the Essex run?' Soge asked.

West turned to him, his mind still on Mobbs. 'What?'

'With Nicky not here?'

'Frankie's got someone in mind,' West said. 'He's talking to him tonight.' He turned and made his way back through the crush of people.

As West left the club a girl with dyed hair and junk

earrings got up on stage and started to belt out the old Nancy Sinatra hit, 'These Boots Are Made For Walking'.

Four

There comes a time at night when a strange silence haunts the ear, when fear has a face. This is a time for those who belong nowhere, who live on the outside of everything.

Mahon parked his car and made his way to meet his next client. As the darkness fell on him he could feel the nearness of rain.

Emma was waiting in the cafe drinking coffee. He glanced through the window before he entered; she was sitting motionless as though she had found a still centre within herself. On the table was a folded newspaper.

As he entered she looked up briefly, but said nothing as he settled at her table. Emma was twenty, her habit had turned from use to abuse, she was living her life without a future; they both knew that she would never see thirty.

Mahon glanced round the cafe; it was shabby and ill-lit. The street girls used it to keep dry and warm when the weather turned bad. He had been here before to meet Emma, but tonight it seemed different: it was the same man behind the counter, his face all corners, there were the same cheap chairs and tables, the same glass ashtrays with some obscure French aperitif advertised on the side, the same bowls of dusty sugar lumps with the odd fly hobbling over them. What was different?

Emma ran a finger round the rim of her cup. 'I'm going to Paris.'

Mahon summoned interest. 'Paris?'

'To see my father.'

Mahon nodded but said nothing.

'Just for the weekend.' Emma picked up her cup and sipped her coffee, then with a half sigh lowered it back to the saucer. 'I visit twice a year.'

Mahon checked a clock on the wall; it had stopped. That was it, the clock was different; it was bigger and older, like the clocks you used to see on the walls of railway station waiting rooms, and like most of them it had stopped.

Emma thought he was listening. 'It's not easy; his new wife's not much older than me.'

Mahon had grown weary of words; most of the time what we say is only a clumsy approximation of what we feel. Everyone wanted to talk and they expected you to listen. People think that a drug dealer is safer than a priest. They say things to you, tell you things they wouldn't dream of telling anyone else. When you're with them they make you feel like you're the most important person around, you're their friend, their fix, their lifeline, you feed their addiction without judgement, you listen to their stories and laugh at their jokes, they show you photographs of past lovers and children they haven't seen for years. Then, when you're gone, they can't even remember what you look like.

Emma looked embarrassed. 'I'm sorry.'

'What for?'

'This personal stuff.'

'Sometimes it's easier to talk to someone like me.'

Emma averted her eyes. 'You don't have to listen. I just need to talk.'

Mahon felt he could reach out and touch her loneliness. Here she was, a beautiful young woman, intelligent, cultured, articulate, in a sleazy back street cafe used by toms, talking to a drug dealer who isn't listening. You have to fall a long way before you reach those airless depths. Mahon pointed to her empty cup. 'Want another?'

She smiled. 'Thank you.'

Mahon went to the counter and ordered the coffees, then returned to the table. He looked at Emma. 'I prefer that face.'

Emma looked at him quizzically.

Mahon sat down. 'When you smile.'

Emma smiled again, briefly embarrassed.

'With a smile like that you could be Irish.'

Emma laughed. 'Half French.'

Mahon shrugged. 'That's better than all English.'

'You'd get on well with my father.'

'He's the French half?'

'Born, raised, educated in Paris.'

'But married English?'

'Beautiful, arrogant and rich.'

'In that order?' Mahon enquired lightly.

They had never talked like this before. Emma was plainly enjoying it. 'My mother hated France.'

This amused Mahon. 'So she married a Frenchman?'

'She could be perverse.'

The man with the cornered face shuffled out from behind his counter with their coffees. He made his way slowly to their table and placed them down carefully.

He pointed to the folded newspaper. 'Are you finished with that?'

A moment of alarm flew like a bird across Emma's face. She dropped a hand on the paper. 'No!'

The poor man drew back as if stung. 'Just asking.' He turned and shuffled back to the security of his counter.

Mahon tried to ease Emma. 'Your mother?'

'What?'

'Your mother. You were saying . . . ?'

'Oh . . . yes . . .' She slowly removed her hand from the newspaper. 'When he proposed she said she would marry him on one condition: that she would never have to go to France. They got married and she never did.'

'What was it that made her feel that way about France?'

'How many devils can dance on a pin?'

'What?'

Emma smiled, remembering. 'When I asked her, that's what she would say, How many devils can dance on a pin?'

'She sounds quite a woman.'

Emma smiled. 'She was – quite a woman.'

Mahon felt awkward.

'She died.'

'I'm sorry.'

Emma repeated it as though to convince herself. 'My mother died.'

For the first time Mahon realised how small and frail Emma was; she had barely any substance, she was almost a ghost.

'She wrote me a letter every day of her last few weeks.'

'Even when you were in the house?'

Emma looked at Mahon amazed. 'How did you know that?'

'My father did the same.'

Emma leaned forward. 'That's extraordinary.'

Mahon looked away; he knew he had broken the rule. He never talked about himself or his family to these people.

'Do you think about him much?'

Mahon nodded. 'Yes.'

'All the time?'

'Yes.'

'Every day?'

'Every day.'

'So do I.' Emma sat back and looked at Mahon.

'Memories,' Mahon said with a hint of regret.

Emma picked up on it. 'I remember reading once that all thought is memory.'

Mahon considered this but said nothing.

Emma opened her bag and took out a packet of cigarettes. 'I sometimes think that I see things through a faulty memory.'

Mahon knew what she meant. 'We all do that.'

Emma opened the packet; it was empty. 'Why? Why do we do it?'

Mahon shrugged. 'The moment we think of the past we pull it into the present.'

'Yes?'

'We're different people from then.'

'Yes?'

'So we adjust the past to fit the present.'

'Yes, but why?'

'I don't think it's a conscious thing.'

Emma put the empty packet in the ashtray. 'It is with me.'

They both felt a moment of unease, didn't really

want to continue this conversation; it was starting to become confessional. Mahon checked his watch.

Emma didn't want him to go but she knew that he would. She reached out and moved the newspaper closer to Mahon. 'Have you got a cigarette?'

Mahon paused for a moment. In the course of their conversation he had quite forgotten why he was there. He dipped a hand in his pocket. 'Sure.' He took out a packet and passed it to her.

'Thanks.' She opened it. Inside were twenty untipped cigarettes spiked with diamorphin, a cross pressed into the tobacco with a thumbnail.

'Keep the packet,' Mahon said.

Emma closed the packet and put it carefully in her bag.

Mahon rose and picked up the newspaper. 'Enjoy Paris.'

She looked at him as he prepared to leave. 'See you when I get back?'

Mahon knew this was not a question but a statement. The only person Emma could depend on was him; she knew she could leave her nightmare at his door.

As he left the cafe Mahon looked back in and watched Emma take out the cigarettes, light one and become lost in that narcotic dead zone all heavy users know about. He opened the newspaper. Inside was his money. He slipped it into a pocket and dropped the paper in a litter bin as he moved off.

Mahon turned down a dark side street making his way back to his car. It was raining, that fine drizzle that can soak you to the skin. For some time he'd had a vague edgy feeling; he sensed that he was being followed, he could feel it on the back of his neck. Then he heard footsteps behind him. He continued, slightly lengthening his stride. The footsteps quickened and closed. Mahon stopped and turned to face two figures caught in a clot of shadow.

They moved into the thin light from a street lamp. The smaller man spoke. 'You Mahon?'

Mahon didn't reply. He could just see the man's face; it was scarred with acne. His voice was flat and nasal.

'Fuck off! This is where the big dog eats.'

Mahon balanced himself for trouble. 'Who would that be?'

The small man was on to Mahon's question like a shark. 'Shut yer crack and listen.'

The big man had hangman's hands and a large bony head like an Easter Island sculpture.

The small man took a step forward. 'Just fuck off you thick Irish cunt, and don't come back.'

Mahon shot out a hand, clamped it round the small man's jaw and dug his fingers into the nerves of his face. The man's eyes lurched with pain.

As the minder moved in Mahon kicked him in the shin. His head came down and Mahon hit him hard and short. He dropped unconscious to the pavement glazed with rain. It was over in seconds. Mahon's fingers were still hooked in the small man's face. He looked at him for some time before he spoke. 'You tell your man I don't want a war. He can work his corner, I'll work mine. There's enough round here for both of us.'

The small man couldn't speak.

Mahon released him. 'You got that?'

There were dented white fingerprints on his face from the pressure of Mahon's grip.

The big man stirred on the wet pavement. The small man glanced down at him as if he still couldn't believe it, then looked back at Mahon.

'You got it?' Mahon repeated.

The small man nodded, not daring to speak.

'Good,' Mahon said, then he turned and walked away. When he got to his car he looked back. The big man was walking unsteadily in the opposite direction, the small man was yapping at his heels like a dog.

Five

Two skull busters wearing black bomber jackets with 'Seaman Securities' on the back were searching a club queue for weapons and drugs. One of them was a heavy-set man with cropped hair and prison tats on his hands. He seemed to enjoy touching up the young girls and intimidating the boys they were with. The other was more civilised, he was just doing his job. It was a job he didn't much care for but at least it was better than standing in line at the SS.

A face who looked like a weasel on speed left the club, slipped past the doormen and moved quickly down the street as a Lexus pulled up and parked outside. Seaman and Connell got out and started up the steps.

The decent doorman saw them. He detached himself from the queue and came across. 'Christ knows what would happen if there was a fire in there; it's already packed and they're still comin'.'

Seaman went to move on. 'That's not our headache.'

The doorman pushed. 'It could be.'

Seaman stopped. If there was any threat to his business he wanted to know about it. 'So tell me.'

'The fire officer was round this morning, warned them. They'll close this place down, Dave.'

Connell glared at him; he didn't like this man. 'Do the fuckin' job.'

The doorman shrugged; he didn't want a row with Connell. With a parting glance he moved back to the queue.

As they walked into the club, Seaman appealed to Connell's better nature. 'He's a thinker.'

'He's a cunt. I don't trust him,' Connell said.

The smile left Seaman's face as he opened the door. 'You're right, get rid of him.'

Inside the club was like the third circle of hell: the lights the sounds all wrap around, the kids dancing their brains out. The kids who had just entered stood around waiting to come up on their pill, waiting for the rush.

Seaman and Connell stood on the fringes mapping the scene. Connell was blimping a young girl with a body that made Madonna look like a stick insect.

Seaman leaned into him. 'You could get five years for what you're thinking.'

Connell grinned. 'Ten.'

Verell approached; he'd been expecting them. He was as smooth as a suppository, dressed in an Armani suit, silk tie and handmade shoes. He looked like a bent solicitor, which is exactly what he had been before he was struck off.

Seaman greeted him. 'You must be fallin' off your wallet?'

Verell panned his head like a slowed electric fan round the packed club. It was like this every night. He knew he was into a little gold mine but greed was his first and second nature; however much he was making he wanted more. His eyes came to rest on Seaman. 'It's a living.'

This wasn't social; Seaman was here on business. 'You wanted a word?'

The music was relentless. Verell pulled a pained face. 'Come up to the office.'

The office was right at the top of the building. It was small and cramped with a desk by the window that looked down on to the tacky shimmer of a south London highstreet. On the desk was a stew of papers and a large mains-powered calculating machine. The club building had once been a small repertory theatre that had seen decades as a bingo hall. The office would have probably been a prop room full of stored pantomime gear and boxes of odds and sods that might have proved useful in almost any production from a drawing room comedy to a Whitehall farce.

The door opened and they entered. Seaman was out of breath from the steep climb. 'I'd forgotten those fuckin' stairs!'

Verell crossed the office to check if he had any messages on his answering machine. 'You get used to it.'

Seaman flopped down in a chair. 'You can get used to cancer!'

There were no messages. Verell turned back to Seaman. 'Hardly anyone comes up here.'

Seaman glanced round the office. 'I can see why.' Every time he came up here it seemed to Dave Seaman that the place was smaller and dustier than the time before. 'I don't know how you can work in this fuckin' rat hole!'

Verell slid a filing cabinet drawer open. 'It does me.'

'All the money you're makin'.'

Verell took a bottle of scotch and two glasses from the drawer. 'I'm going to be out of here in three years.'

Seaman took one of the glasses from him. 'Three years?'

Verell poured him a drink. 'With a suitcase full of money.'

'Very nice too.'

Connell hadn't been here before. He leant on the desk and looked down into the high street at the queue of kids waiting to enter the club. 'Look at 'em! Fifteen, sixteen? Fuckin' bodies on 'em!'

Verell poured Connell a drink and handed it to him.

Connell grinned. 'I think I'll come and work this door fer a few nights.'

Seaman noticed that Verell wasn't drinking. 'Ulcer?'

'It's killing me.'

'You look like shit.'

Verell put the bottle back in the cabinet and closed it. 'Thanks.'

Seaman sipped his scotch. 'So? What's up?'

There was a moment of reflection in Verell's eyes as though he was trying to organise his thoughts. 'Well . . . the nub of it is that there are certain people want to close me down.'

'You've had that right from the off.'

'This is different.'

'How?'

'These people . . . one in particular . . . a man called Harle . . .'

Seaman knew the man. 'That fuckin' pencil neck!'

Verell took out a pack of Camels. 'He's got a lot of bite in the council.'

'He's been at you since you opened?'

'That's right.'

Seaman shrugged. 'You're still open.'

Verell shook the cigarettes up and offered Seaman one. 'Now he's trying to nail me.'

Seaman looked at the cigarettes and remembered his breathless climb. 'Ah fuck it!' He took one and lit it. 'And fuck him!'

'That's what I want to talk about.'

Seaman knew that Verell was a clever man; he always seemed to be on the next page. 'Fucking him?'

Verell took out a gold Dunhill and lit his cigarette. 'Professionally.'

'How?'

'I'm going to need Pauli's help.'

Seaman smiled. 'It'll cost.'

'If it works, it's worth it.'

'You want to talk to Pauli?'

'Can you set it up?'

'When?'

'This week?'

'It's that bad?'

'Worse.'

'I'll see what I can do.'

The weasel lurked in the shadows of a shop entrance, using a mobile, his eyes flicking up and down the street for any sign of friction. 'Look, listen to me, now listen. I don't give a monkey's what it is, I can sell these fuckin' trainspotters anything, powdered rat shit, just get it to me!' He switched the mobile off, folded it, dropped it back in his pocket and prepared to wait.

A new BMW coupe turned into the street with its lights switched off, and pulled up. Davey Tolman lowered his window and looked into the shadow of the shop doorway. At seventeen Davey was already into his own action.

The weasel stepped out casting furtive glances up and down the street and moved to the car. 'Where you bin?'

'What?'

'I've bin here fuckin' hours!'

Davey checked his watch. 'Twenty minutes.'

The weasel was well put out. 'Time's money to me!'

Davey was ultra cool. 'Money? You want ter talk about money?'

The weasel backed off. 'It's fuckin' cold out here.'

Davey lit a cigarette and blew smoke at him. 'You're into me for eleven hundred.' He picked up a small package from the passenger seat and passed it to the dealer. 'That makes it one four, right?'

The weasel stuffed the packet inside his jacket. 'I'll square up with you Monday.'

Davey wanted this right. 'Monday?'

The weasel was eager to be away. 'Where will I find you?'

'I'll find you,' Davey said.

The weasel knew he meant this in more ways than one. 'You know I'm good for it.'

Davey gave him a warning look. 'You better be.'

The weasel was offended. 'Fuck off, Davey. You know I always settle.'

Davey lit a cigarette. 'I hear you owe Dave Seaman.'

The weasel didn't want to be reminded of this. He mumbled something that Davey didn't catch.

Davey smiled. 'I can hear your arse quacking.' He dropped the car into gear. 'Fourteen hundred, right?'

The dealer nodded.

'Monday.'

'Piss off!'

Davey drove off leaving the weasel to ponder his future. He didn't switch the car lights on until he reached the end of the road.

The weasel walked quickly back past the queue of kids and started up the steps of the club, gliding past the security men as though he was invisible. As he ran up the last few steps he almost bumped into Seaman coming out with Verell.

The dealer froze.

Seaman fixed him with a look that would freeze alcohol. 'What are you doin' here?'

The weasel turned to run but Connell grabbed him by the scruff of his neck. 'Come here you snaky little bastard!'

The queue of kids was watching; it was bad for business. Verell turned to Seaman. 'Not here, Dave.'

Seaman nodded to Connell who dragged the dealer down the stairs to the parked car, opened the back door, bundled him in, got in with him and slammed the door.

Seaman followed them down leaving Verell standing nervously on the steps. He got into the driver's seat, started the car and pulled away with a whimper of tyres.

In the back of the car Connell had the weasel by the throat. His face was the colour of a peeled egg.

As he drove, Seaman half turned and talked over his shoulder. 'You work my clubs, you know the deal, you pay your taxes.'

Connell increased his grip on the weasel's throat; his eyes started to pop.

Seaman powered the big car through red traffic lights. 'You owe me money you fuckin' maggot!'

The night club had only recently opened; it still smelt of fresh paint and newly laid carpet. The interior was loosely based on a famous old twenties club in New York where the pretentious gathered. There were large sepia photographs of it in thin gold frames hanging on the walls.

The clone in London was meant to be ultra chic, a handy hang out for celebrities. On a lit glass floor couples were dancing badly to a small Latin combo, but underneath the veneer of bamboo and buttoned velvet it was really just another club. They were opening every month and the clientele, the sort of people with too much money who kept boredom at bay by being seen at places like this, were fickle. When the next club opened these publicity hungry self-promoters were gone, chasing the gossip column journalists who always got a free ride on the opening night.

Pauli West and Dave Seaman were sat at one of the tables, smoking cigars and drinking vintage champagne. Seaman had told West about his visit to Verell. West knew him. When he was a solicitor he had acted for him on a number of occasions. He took more than the occasional liberty with procedures and written rules of conduct; few were surprised when he faced disbarment.

'I've never liked the man.'

Seaman looked at West. 'I know.'

'Scheming little cunt!'

'You don't have to like him to take his money.'

'Do you know what he's after?'

'He wants Councillor Harle off his back.'

West reacted. 'Harle?'

'The fuckin' magic Christian!'

'He's as straight as Verell is crooked.'

'I reckon Verell's got something on him.'

Suddenly West seemed interested. 'Did he say that?'

'Not straight out.'

'And he wants a meet?'

'What harm can it do?'

'This club of his?'

'He's makin' a bundle, Pauli.'

'Maybe he needs a partner?'

Seaman grinned. 'That's what I was thinking.'

'To take care of things.'

'Maybe you might suggest that to him?'

West didn't often smile. 'Maybe I might.'

They made a point of ending their conversation as they saw a good-looking woman, long dark hair and darker eyes, approach their table.

She'd been to the powder room. Fran was Ray Tolman's wife. She slipped into the seat beside West.

He sensed something wrong. 'What's up?'

Fran shook her head. 'Nothing.'

West knew her too well. 'Someone say something?'

Fran took cigarettes from her purse. 'No.'

West glanced round the club. 'You sure?'

Fran lit a cigarette. 'Half the women in there are bumping up!'

West relaxed. 'Cocaine with tequila chasers.'

Seaman smiled. 'It's on the menu.' He lifted the bottle of champagne from the bucket and filled Fran's half-empty glass.

Fran picked up her glass. 'It's so sad.' She looked slowly round at the faces. 'Some of them are so young.' Fran's mobile rang in her purse. She took it out and switched on. 'Hello?' She smiled. 'Ray!' She glanced at West. 'I'm out with Pauli and Dave . . . yeah . . . a new club just opened . . .'

As Fran talked to her husband in prison one of the club management, a young good-looking guy with a moustache like a file of ants under his nose, made his way across to their table and had a discreet word with West. 'I'm sorry sir. There's a strict rule against mobile phones.'

Without looking at him, West slipped a step of money from his pocket, peeled off a fifty and pushed it into his hand. 'Emergency.'

Six

Mahon pushed up into the affluent deadness of west London. He was eating a late-night supermarket sandwich. It was damp and tasteless.

Something caught his eye in the rear view mirror: a police car was coming up fast. He checked his speed then laid the sandwich on the passenger seat, slowed and stopped at red lights.

The police car pulled alongside.

Mahon had learned a trick or two from an old dealer in ways to offset police suspicion. He deliberately turned and looked into the car, meeting the tired eyes of one of the patrolling officers. They were the eyes of a man cut off from the soul of the city.

Mahon knew that his look had been long enough. He turned back as the lights changed.

The police car accelerated ahead.

Mahon pulled away slowly and reached for the sandwich. He had never liked west London. There was something about it, something not quite right. It was too calm, too ordered, people lived lives that excluded the accidental. He preferred the anarchy of the East End; the carnivorous streets, a stain of words on every wall. In west London they didn't care enough about anything to write it on a wall.

He parked his car outside an apartment block that overlooked the park.

The lift opened and Mahon stepped out into a carpeted hallway. He walked to a door at the end, rang the bell and waited.

There was movement inside, a spy-hole lit, the door was unlocked and unchained then opened by Beth.

She was thirty-nine, looked thirty-five, swore she was thirty-two. Details of her body pushed through the soft silk of a saffron kimono with an eighteenth-century Taniguchi Buson haiku embroidered across one breast, *The plum trees bloom – and pleasure women buy new sashes in a brothel room.*

Beth was halfway through her make-up. She turned and started back down the hallway. 'You've caught me with half a face on.'

Mahon entered, closed the door and followed her.

Beth stood in the open doorway of the bedroom. 'I'm late. Can you give me a lift to the Hilton?'

She settled on a stool in front of her make-up table, checked her face in the mirror. 'I won't be long.'

Mahon took out two gram wraps of cocaine. 'Your two, but I've got a spare quarter if you're interested?' He took out the bag meant for Hollander.

Beth looked at his reflection in the mirror. 'How much?'

'Two and a half.'

It was a generous price. Beth turned and pointed

behind him to a small bedside chest. 'In the drawer there.'

Mahon moved to it and slid open the drawer. Inside was a step of notes. He lifted the money out and peeled off five fifties. All the notes were neatly faced. As he went to return the money he saw a small handgun at the back of the drawer. It surprised him but he said nothing. He closed the drawer and moved back to Beth, placing the bag of cocaine on the make-up table.

She glanced at it. 'I'm going to need that.' She opened a box and started to fit contact lenses. 'I've got some fat German banker waiting for me. He'll fuck me then squeal about the price – they always do.'

Mahon cased the room: warm pastel walls, framed Degas ballet prints, smoke-pink carpet, over-dainty taffeta curtains looped in a cotton rope. The fitted wardrobe had a flesh-tinted mirror as though Beth needed reassurance of her beauty as she watched the years cross her face.

Beth saw him in her mirror. 'You haven't been in here before.'

Mahon was embarrassed at being caught looking. He glanced at her reflection in the mirror. 'No.'

'Nor has any other man,' she said, turning slowly to face him.

'In here I feel clean.' She stood and faced Mahon, untied the kimono and opened it. 'Think I've got another five years?'

Mahon didn't reply straight away. He ran his eyes over her body like hands. She had put on weight since he had known her, her breasts were starting to sag, there were stretch marks on her belly from a baby she'd had that was stillborn.

She looked at him. 'Well?'

'At least.' Mahon said.

Beth wrapped the kimono back round her. 'That's what I like about the Irish.' She smiled. 'They know how to lie.'

Seven

Nicky Mobbs thought he was safe. He knew half of London was looking for him but Nicky was a mug punter at heart; he did love to push the odds. He'd heard about the heavy faces hiding out in Spain, slipping back into the country to have a meal at their favourite restaurant just to give the filth the finger. Nicky thought that was top drawer, the ultimate fuck off. The thing that separates the everyday villain from a face was this lack of respect for anyone but other faces. Pauli West wasn't the filth; with them you at least got a cup of tea and a phone call. With Pauli it was rough justice that could be terminal. But then Nicky was convinced, as only dreamers full of delusions can be, that he lived a charmed life.

So there was Nicky in his favourite Italian restaurant, having a nice meal and a bottle of Barolo with a pretty woman he'd picked up on the plane coming over, when in walks a nightmare.

Jimmy Ryan sat down at their table. He picked up Nicky's glass of wine, tasted it, then turned to Nicky. 'How much this cost?'

Nicky could see Pete Soge standing in a small passage where they hung the coats. J.W. was outside.

Even when he was behaving himself, Jimmy Ryan had something of the psychopath about him. It was his eyes, you see those eyes in the queer place. The woman sat rigid, a piece of veal on the end of her fork somewhere on the way to her mouth.

Nicky thought he could talk himself safe. 'I tried to ring Pauli.'

Jimmy took another sip of wine and turned to the woman. 'Very nice.'

He ran the back of his finger down her bare arm.

The woman lowered the fork to her plate with a cry of fright that was hardly more than a breath.

Ryan turned back to Mobbs. 'We've bin lookin' for you, Nicky.'

Mobbs glanced towards the back of the restaurant but he knew there was no escape. He turned back to Ryan to front it out. 'I've only just got back.'

Ryan slowly poured the wine over Nicky's food. 'Been away?'

Nicky Mobbs looked down at the floating mess on his plate. 'Ireland.' Drops of wine like spots of blood had fallen on the white linen tablecloth. 'With my brother.'

Ryan leant across, reached into Nicky Mobbs' jacket, hooked out his wallet, opened it, slipped out some cash, folded it and with a smile slid it under the woman's plate.

The waiters were casting anxious glances at the table but they were in no hurry to get involved.

J.W. had moved into the restaurant. A car pulled up outside and stood ticking over.

Ryan glanced out at the waiting car then turned back to Nicky Mobbs. 'You fit?'

Mobbs was still trying to front it out. 'There was no need for this sort of heavy shit, Jimmy.'

Ryan got up and lifted Mobbs up by his tie.

They walked to the door. By now everyone in the restaurant was watching. Ryan passed Nicky Mobbs on to Soge and J.W., who took him out to the car. Ryan couldn't resist it; he turned back to his ready-made audience in the restaurant and gave them a verse and chorus of 'My Way'.

The boarded-up municipal indoor swimming pool was in a narrow side street off a main road that was depressing to drive down. Most of the shops seemed to be closed or close to closing with permanent 'Sale' notices blazed across the windows. The whole district seemed to be plagued with melancholy. Somehow it had missed the eighties boom. There were no nice little ethnic restaurants, no bookshops, no arcade haute couture, no cafes with canopies and tables outside, just cheap shoe shops with racks of reject shoes, a drab betting shop with dead flies and fading blown-up photographs of dog racing in the window, and the pubs, one on every corner, appeared to be jaundiced in the sodium yellow streetlight.

The car drew up. Ryan got out and went to the door of the swimming pool and unlocked it. Pete Soge and J.W. dragged Nicky Mobbs from the car, still protesting. 'What the fuck is all this about?'

Soge gave him a little dig in the side that knocked the wind out of him.

J.W. tried to calm it down. 'Easy, Pete.'

Soge turned to him. 'We've had mouth all the way from the restaurant. I'm sick of listening.'

Jimmy Ryan had gone into the swimming pool. Soge went in after him leaving Mobbs with J.W.

Inside was as black as a badger's arse.

Soge heard Ryan's voice. 'The lights are here somewhere.'

Soge took out his Zippo and lit it. The flickering flame only penetrated the darkness so far. Ryan felt along the wall like a blind man for the light switches.

Soge followed him. 'Hurry up, it's getting hot!'

Ryan found the switches and turned the lights on.

'Fuck it!' Soge dropped his lighter and tried to shake the burning from his fingers.

The pre-war pool had been closed for over ten years. It was in an advanced state of decay. Pauli West had bought it at auction. He knew that one day soon, with the creeping gentrification of surrounding areas, this part of the city would be on the up and he would be holding a sizeable piece of property bang in the middle. The land the swimming pool stood on would be worth a fortune. Soge recovered his lighter and walked down the dimly lit corridor followed by Ryan. Their heels clacked on the cracked black-and-white diamond tiles, every sound echoing through the cavernous old building.

Soge clapped his hands. 'Listen to that echo.'

Ryan looked around. 'I used ter come here as a kid.'

Soge grinned. 'Bet you pissed in the pool.'

They pushed through heavy mahogany doors that creaked and then hissed shut behind them.

Jimmy loved it here. There was just something about a derelict swimming pool that appealed to his gothic imagination. He moved down the steps into the blue-and-white tiled pit of the empty pool that dropped away steeply at one end.

Soge stood on the side watching him.

Jimmy started to daintily swim down the pool;

halfway down he switched to backstroke. He looked
up at Soge and grinned. 'Esther fuckin' Williams!'

Soge followed him along the edge of the pool.
'Who's she?'

Jimmy stopped swimming in disgust. 'You don't
know who Esther Williams is?'

Soge shrugged. 'No.'

Jimmy Ryan started swimming again. 'She was a
film star, always in the water. Great body. I could've
shagged her silly!'

J.W. entered the pool area with Nicky Mobbs. 'What
are we going to do with him?'

A rusting metal stacking chair with a torn canvas
seat had been thrown into the empty pool. Ryan picked
it up, walked to the middle of the pool and placed it
down. 'We wait for Pauli.'

Eight

Mahon dropped Beth off then made his way up to the north London badlands. He walked down a dark street with several shabby hotels in it used by the girls who worked the district. He entered one with a flickering fluorescent sign over the door.

The entrance lobby was empty. As he made his way towards the stairs he passed a dingy office, the door half open. He glanced in.

The night clerk, a fat man with the face of a rapist, was slouched in an armchair stroking a cat on his lap and watching a game show on a portable television.

The stairs creaked as Mahon started to climb them.

He arrived at the second floor and turned down a dimly lit corridor choked with dust. The wallpaper was peeling, flakes of ceiling white had fallen like snow on the worn carpet. He got to a door, checked the number and knocked. It was opened a crack and an eye peered out, then the door opened wider and Mahon slipped in.

Frankie Pitillo closed and locked the door as Mahon made his way across the grim room and stood at the window staring down into the street. He saw a young tom, her pale face pinched and sullen, emerging from a hotel opposite, straightening her skirt as she went back to work the meatrack.

Pitillo crossed to Mahon, who turned and took out a fold of notes. 'Forty two hundred, right?' He wanted to be gone. 'I'm in a hurry.'

Pitillo wasn't a man you could hurry. 'That's how I ended up in a peter sorting through my shit on a newspaper with a fork.' His eyes never left the money. 'It ain't easy inside with a habit. Ended up in a detox cell.'

Mahon didn't want to hear this. 'You got my stuff?'

Pitillo took a package wrapped round with brown plastic tape from a poacher's pocket inside his coat, and passed it to Mahon who gave him the money. He started to count it with nicotine-coated fingers.

Mahon took out a penknife and opened the blade. He cut a small slit in the package and squeezed out some of the powder. He licked a finger and tested it.

'That shit'll set the standard. They ain't tasted nothing like that on the street fer months.' Pitillo continued counting. 'You can step all over it.'

Mahon ignored him, took out a roll of tape, tore a piece off and repaired the package, then dropped it in a pocket and went to leave.

Pitillo had finished counting. He looked up at Mahon. 'I'll take another twenty.'

Mahon was halfway to the door. He knew the money was right. He turned back. 'You better count it again.'

Pitillo held out a hand. 'Twenty pounds,' he smiled showing sharp uneven teeth stained like a urinal, 'fer the room.'

Mahon moved back across the room towards him in a way that Frankie saw as threatening. A knife slid from his sleeve, he pressed a button, the blade caught the light as it dropped.

Mahon stopped and looked at Frankie, then at the knife. The air between them thickened. 'Twenty?'

Even with a chib Frankie didn't fancy banging head with this man. He tried to talk himself safe. 'Goin' rate fer the girls.'

Mahon looked round the scuzzy room. It was cramped and dirty and stank of mould. 'For this?'

Pitillo shrugged. 'Economics. About a pound a poke fer them.'

Mahon dipped a hand in a pocket and produced a twenty pound note. 'I'd like a receipt.'

Pitillo was thrown.

Mahon knew a smile would ease the tension. 'VAT.'

Pitillo raised the knife and pressed the button; the blade dropped back into the handle and he put it away. 'I like a sense of humour.' He took the twenty. 'I like you big man; you turn up on time, don't shit me, the money checks, you collect the product and you're gone.' The muscles of his face relaxed. 'Very professional.'

Mahon stood listening to him.

Pitillo took out a packet of cigarettes and lit one. 'I've been talking to my people about you.'

Mahon let him talk.

'You interested in a little collection job?'

Mahon hadn't expected this. 'That depends.'

'On what?'

'The money and the risk.'

'A clean thousand or a half of the top.'

'Of what?' Mahon asked.

'Pharmaceutical, coming in from Holland.'

It sounded useful, but Mahon was cautious. 'And the catch?'

Pitillo smoked nervously. 'No catch.'

Mahon couldn't resist a wry smile. 'You must like me.'

Pitillo pushed hard to sell it to the big Irishman. 'My man's sick, short notice, I can't go.'

'Why not?' Mahon asked.

'Please,' he shook his head as if it was all too complex, 'don't ask.'

Mahon knew that Frankie had more than a passing acquaintance with the Drug Squad; the fact that he had an expensive habit didn't help.

'When is this?' Mahon asked.

'Wednesday night.' Pitillo looked at Mahon for a reaction. 'It's yours if you want it.'

Mahon considered for a moment then looked hard at Pitillo. 'If it goes bad I'm gonna find you, Frankie.'

Pitillo was about to put the fold of money away. 'It can't go bad. We've done it a dozen times – it's fuckin' perfect.' He thumbed off Mahon's twenty and handed it back to him. 'Forget the room. Let's get out of this shit pit and get a drink.'

The battle stank of disinfectant, spilled beer and stale cigarette smoke. It was a rough house full of faces where the closed world of criminal gossip was exchanged. Four young hounds were playing a noisy game of pool, Mahon and Pitillo were sat at a table well away from them going through the details of the job. Mahon was nursing a whisky, Frankie was drinking lager and chain-smoking.

They weren't aware that they were being watched.

Billy Binns was in his early twenties but his ice-cream face lied about his age; he looked sixteen. He sat

on a stool at the bar drinking from a bottle of Rolling
Rock. He never took his eyes from them.

Frankie took out a note and held it out to Mahon.
'I'm goin' fer a waz. Why don't you go and get another
round?'

Mahon pointed to his drink. 'This'll do me.'

Frankie grinned and got up to go to the toilet. 'You
sure you're Irish?'

Mahon reluctantly took the money. 'Lager?'

Pitillo moved away from the table. 'Nah, fuckin'
stuff does my plumbing in. Large Grouse.'

Binns watched him make his way to the toilet. At
first he hadn't been sure but now he was satisfied it
was Frankie Pitillo. He left the half-drunk bottle on the
jump, slid from the stool and weaved his way through
the crowd to the door.

Billy Binns took out a mobile and thumbed a number as
he walked down the street. He slipped into the shadow
of a jeweller's shop doorway, talking. 'That Frankie
Pitillo, he's in the Star . . . yeah, yeah it's him, I'm
sure it's him . . . no, he's with someone . . . no, never
seen him before . . . Irish . . . I heard him order their
drinks, didn' I?' He listened carefully to the instructions
he was given. 'Yeah . . . yeah . . . okay . . . right.' He
stepped from the shadow folding the mobile, dropped
it in a pocket and made his way back to the battle.

Mahon and Pitillo had finished their business. They had
moved on to more personal stuff.

Frankie was a talker. 'I was on what was supposed to
be a drug-free wing, a rehabilitation wing.' Pitillo's laugh
was like a dog barking. 'That was a joke.' He dragged
on his cigarette, smoke hung round his head. 'Anyway,
one night I was at bingo. Must've bin scratchin' like

hell, a screw was right on me. They piss tested me, it was bound ter be on top . . . had to wait a week for the results but I knew . . . eyes like fuckin' microdots.'

Prison stories bored Mahon but he listened patiently waiting for an opportunity to leave.

Pitillo looked at him. 'You bin away?'

The sudden question took Mahon by surprise. 'What?'

'Inside.'

'Yeah.'

'Where?'

'Military prison.'

Pitillo was sympathetic. 'I hear they can be bastard places.'

Mahon finished his whisky. 'I've got to go.'

Pitillo wanted to know more. 'What'yer pull?'

'Three years.'

'Me, most I've done is a two,' Frankie said, taking the cigarette from between his thin lips. 'Fuck, it felt like ten.'

Time weighed just as heavy on Mahon. 'I've got someone waiting.'

'What yer do?'

Mahon could see that Pitillo wasn't going to let him go without knowing. 'Assaulted a civilian.'

'Why?'

'He called me an Irish pig.'

'Big guy?'

Mahon got up to leave. 'He thought so.'

Mahon and Pitillo left the pub and walked slowly down the street. The lights were out, it was as dark as the inside of a cow.

Binns slipped out and followed them.

Mahon stopped and pointed across the road. 'Want a lift?'

Pitillo grinned. 'Nah, gonna get me knob polished.'
He pointed vaguely down the road. 'She lives local.'

Mahon was relieved that at last he was rid of Pitillo.
'Wednesday night then.'

Frankie had become more impressed with Mahon
the more he knew about him. This big Irishman could
prove very useful. 'My people are connected. You play
it right you could be on the up.'

They went their different ways; Frankie continued
on down the street with a scuttling crab-like gait,
Mahon crossed the road.

As he went to turn down the side street where his car
was parked he heard a disturbance. He turned and saw
Pitillo, a blanket over his head, being dragged towards
a waiting car by three men. A back door was open,
the engine revving. Without streetlights all that Mahon
could see were silhouettes.

He ran across the road narrowly missing being run
down by a rusting Transit van. The driver pumped his
horn and cursed him.

One of the three men had a baseball bat. As Mahon
came on he swung at him. Mahon avoided it and hit
him hard. As the man went down Mahon grabbed the
bat and wrenched it from his hands.

The driver punched his door open and went to get out
to deal with him, but Mahon kicked the door. It smashed
back shattering the window on the driver's head.

Seeing this unexpected explosion of violence, Billy
Binns lurked in the shadows. He didn't want to know.

Mahon rammed the end of the bat into the back of
the car, breaking the jaw of one of the men holding
Pitillo, then he dropped it, reached in and dragged
Frankie out.

The driver, a sheet of blood down his face, was
back behind the wheel. He revved the engine hard,

dropped into gear and wheelspun the car away, the door flapping, the uninjured men in the back desperately trying to close it.

Mahon helped Pitillo to his feet.

Frankie was shaken. He looked at Mahon. 'Did you see 'em?'

Mahon watched the car disappear down the road then shook his head. 'It was too dark.'

Pitillo ran the back of his hand across his bloody mouth. 'Fuckin' reptiles!'

The man Mahon hit had scrambled to his feet and was running off down the street. Binns was long gone. In the distance Mahon could hear the unmistakable whine of a police siren.

He half lifted the limping Pitillo across the road and down the side street to his parked car and leant him back against it. The side of his face was swelling. He unlocked the car and got Pitillo into the passenger seat.

Mahon drove as fast as he could through a maze of backstreets, not knowing where he was, putting as much distance as he could between them and the police.

Pitillo was slumped beside Mahon, feeling all squeezed out. He turned but found it difficult to talk with his swollen mouth. 'I won't forget this.'

Mahon was concentrating on his driving.

Frankie lit a cigarette. 'You could've fucked off.' He dragged deep on the smoke. He couldn't work out this big, almost silent Irishman. 'Why didn't yer?'

Mahon shrugged the logic of it. 'I'm into half of pure. Cut right, sold right, I can make real money.'

'That all you think about, money?'

'No.'

'No?'

Mahon dropped a gear. 'Sometimes I think about sex.'

Pitillo was never quite sure when Mahon was serious. Mahon kept his eyes on the splash of headlights.

Pitillo dragged on his cigarette. 'You got a woman?'

Mahon shook his head.

Pitillo couldn't believe this. The big Irishman was a good-looking man, he could have any woman he wanted. 'No?'

Mahon braked hard to turn a tight corner. 'I've got a dog.'

Frankie Pitillo tried to laugh but it hurt. He turned to Mahon. 'I can handle the women, but money . . .' he blew ash from the end of his cigarette, 'when I've got money I jus' spunk it, it's gone. That's the way I am.'

Mahon looked briefly at Frankie. He was starting to like him but knew he could never trust him.

Frankie's inky eyes had become serious. 'I used ter rent when I was young and pretty— it was good money. That's how I got into heroin.' He turned away and stared out of the window. 'After that I'd fuck a dog for fourpence.'

They drove on in silence.

Nine

Mahon sat at the club bar with a drink. He'd had to put a tie on to get in. He watched West and Seaman with the woman in a mirrored wall behind the bar. They were respectful and protective of her, but when she stopped pretending that she was having a good time she appeared on the edge of despair, as though she was a prisoner of these men.

A pushy barman came up to him and pointed to his drink. 'You going to nurse that all night?'

Mahon ignored the sarcasm. He downed the drink and pushed the empty glass at the barman. 'Bushmills.'

The barman picked the glass up. 'Ice?'

'No ice.'

'Water?'

Mahon turned his eyes back to the mirrored wall. 'No water.'

The barman moved down the bar to search for the bottle of Irish. J.W. entered the club and approached the table. He bent over to talk quietly to West.

'We've got Nicky Mobbs.'

West got up and stepped away from the table. 'Where?'

J.W. followed him. 'At the baths.' J.W. was edgy. 'He's screamin' blue fuckin' murder. I didn't really want to leave him with Jimmy; he's in one of his mad moods. He'll kill him, Pauli.'

West returned to the table, gathered up his cigarettes and lighter and turned to Seaman. 'Where's your car?'

Seaman got up and took keys from a pocket. 'Outside.'

West turned back to J.W. 'Look after Fran. See that she gets back safe.'

J.W. nodded. 'Okay, but watch Jimmy.' He tapped his temple. 'He's not too tightly wrapped.'

West bent down to Fran and had a parting word with her. 'J will drive you home when you're ready.'

Fran knew better than to ask questions.

Mahon watched West and Seaman leave, then he saw J.W. slide into the seat next to Fran. He offered her a cigarette and lit it.

'Seen Ray lately?'

Fran pulled a mock-jade ashtray shaped like hand closer. 'Last week. Special visit, with his solicitor.'

'How was he?'

'Lost some weight.'

'Working out?'

'Certainly looks fit.'

'Pauli said they haven't given you a date yet.'

'Date?'

'For the new trial.'

Fran's face emptied. 'No, they haven't.'

'What does Ray reckon?'

There was a hollowness in her reply. 'You know Ray, always the optimist.'

'What about you?' J.W. asked.

Fran showed a shard of despair. She knew she could with J.W.; he was closer to her than the rest. It wouldn't go further. 'I don't think I can face fifteen years on my own.'

J.W. was alarmed. He moved his head closer to Fran. 'Don't let Pauli hear you say that.'

Fran dropped her cigarette in the ashtray. 'Take me home. I'm tired.'

J.W. got up and eased the table back.

Fran picked up her bag and stepped out.

Mahon followed them closely in the mirror as they made their way from the club. He was not aware of the barman watching him watching them.

The barman put Mahon's drink down on a bar mat. 'Beautiful woman.' Mahon turned to him but said nothing. The barman glanced across the club at Fran, who by now was almost out of sight. He tried to make the question sound casual. 'Do you know her?' When Mahon didn't reply the barman darted a glance at the mirror. 'The way you've been watching her, I thought you must know her.'

Mahon was only mildly annoyed by the prying barman; his mind was on other things. He took out a ten and dropped it on the bar beside the drink, got off the stool and walked away.

The barman called after him. 'What about your drink?'

Mahon ignored him and continued walking.

The barman watched Mahon leave the club, then with a sly glance round he dropped a hand on the note, slid it from the bar and slipped it in his pocket.

Ten

The powerful saloon eased through the city, its head-lights bisecting the darkness. J.W. was a good driver; fast but safe, his movements fluid and co-ordinated.

Fran sat beside him, her dead face the map of her emotions. She stared out silently as the outskirts of the city smeared past and the quiet elegance of the west London suburbs started to appear. Rain flecked the window.

Fran was half in, half out of her haunted past. In the eighteen years she had been with Ray, she had not lived a normal life. She had always been close to some extreme, and had often wondered what the rules of a normal married woman's life were. She doubted that they included never asking questions. There had been love, yes of course there had been love, especially in those first years when Davey was a child, but love, whatever else it is, is interior, something held inside to be drawn on when there is nothing else.

Ray was a generous man; she had the large house, the Mercedes, an unlimited wardrobe, accounts at fashionable stores, expensive foreign holidays. On the surface it would appear she wanted for nothing, but her life had become a poison that smelled like a perfume.

J.W. could see that she was blue. He tried to start a conversation. 'How's the boy?'

Fran turned slowly from the window to face him.

J.W. smiled affably. 'How is he?'

'Davey?'

'I haven't seen him for a while.'

J.W. was the only one of Pauli West's people that Fran liked, the only one that she could bear to be with. She knew he was trying to help. 'I hardly ever see him. He doesn't come home for days.'

'How old is he now?'

'Seventeen.'

This genuinely surprised him. 'Seventeen?'

She found herself becoming solemn. 'I was married at seventeen.'

J.W. tried to keep the conversation light. 'Good-looking lad.'

Those half-buried memories were there again, floating through Fran's mind. 'I was sixteen when I met Ray. He was the best-looking man I'd ever seen. I couldn't believe he was interested in me; he could have had any girl he wanted.' She paused, wondering where her life had gone. 'I met him at sixteen, was married at seventeen, Davey was born ten months later.' It all seemed so ordered but meaningless. 'I've never known anything else but Ray, his friends, the life he lives.' Defeated by the memories, Fran turned back to the window. The rain had lessened. 'It's been half of half a life for me.'

The car swept into a driveway that led to a large house.

All the lights were out. It stopped at the front door and
J.W. switched the ignition off.

Fran got out and looked back into the car. 'Thanks J.'

J.W. was worried about Fran, worried about what
she'd been saying. He looked out at her. 'Be careful of Pauli, what you say. You know how he feels
about Ray.'

She reached in her bag for the house keys.

'How close they are,' J.W. added.

Fran ran the word over her tongue testing it. 'Close.'

J.W. reacted. 'You know what I mean.'

Fran realised that J.W. had mistaken this for a question. She knew the word didn't even start to describe
the relationship. She looked at J.W. 'It's like having
two husbands, being married to both of them.'

'Just be careful; Pauli doesn't miss much,' J.W. said,
starting the car. 'You know what he's like. You know
what he can be like; there's no talking to him. He gets
things all twisted.'

Fran lowered her voice. 'He frightens me, J.'

J.W. knew what she meant. 'He's certainly not a
man to get on the wrong side of.' He reached out and
took her hand. 'Just be careful, Frannie.'

He was the only one who called her 'Frannie'. She
liked it. She squeezed his hand. 'Thanks.'

Fran closed the car door then turned and walked up
the steps. As she slid the key in the lock she heard the
car moving slowly down the gravel drive. She turned
and watched it pull into the road. When she was sure it
was gone, Fran took the key from the lock and walked
back down the drive. She stopped at the entrance and
checked the street in both directions, then slipped into
the night.

Eleven

Seaman's car pulled up in the narrow side street. The lights were switched off. West and Seaman stepped from it, walked down to the swimming pool and entered.

Seaman turned to West. 'What are you gonna do with this dump, Pauli? Pull it down?'

West stopped and turned to Seaman. 'You wait here. Make sure we're not disturbed.' He pushed through a heavy door into the pool; it hissed shut behind him.

Nicky Mobbs was wired by his ankles and wrists to the chair. His face was badly marked; red weals stood out on his pale skin like lipstick on a paper cup. The air crackled with latent violence. Mobbs looked up as West entered. When he saw him his face flushed with relief and he called out, 'Thank Christ you're here, Pauli.' He glanced at Jimmy Ryan, who was sitting on the frayed coconut matting at the end of the spring board, his legs dangling over the empty pool. 'Look what that maniac's done ter me. Look at my face.'

Ryan snatched a gun from his belt and punched it at Mobbs. 'I'm gonna fuck you where you breathe!'

West turned sharply to Ryan. 'Put it away, Jimmy.'

Ryan got angrily to his feet. 'He's cattled you, Pauli.'

West's voice tightened. 'Put it away.'

Reluctantly Ryan stuck the gun in his belt and walked back along the board. He stepped off and crossed to West. 'He's in with Venner. He's Venner's man.'

Mobbs heard this. 'He needs his fuckin' head feelin', Pauli.'

West turned to Mobbs. 'You've got a lot of explaining to do.'

Mobbs appeared genuinely upset. He looked up angrily at West. 'I hate Venner just as much as you do. I wouldn't take his hand if I was drownin'.'

West moved slowly down the steps into the pool, walked across to Mobbs and stood looking down at him. 'Did you know it only takes four inches of water to drown a man?'

Mobbs knew that Pauli West was dangerous when he was in this quiet mood.

'I read it somewhere,' West observed vaguely.

Mobbs dragged the conversation back to Venner. 'He's a filthy grassin' . . .' a gout of phlegm rose in his throat and he spat it out. 'He's a fuckin' dog, Pauli.'

West ignored this outburst from Mobbs. 'We've been looking for you, Nicky . . .' he walked slowly round behind him, 'all week.'

'I've bin in Ireland,' Mobbs said, turning his head as far as he could to try and keep his eyes on West. 'With my brother. He was ill.'

West looked at him stone-faced. 'You didn't say? You didn't tell anyone?'

'It was an emergency. I got the first flight out. I didn't have time to tell no one,' said Mobbs.

Ryan stalked along the side of the pool listening to them. 'You lyin' piece of dirt!'

Soge walked along the other side. 'We checked the airports.'

Mobbs turned sharply to Soge. 'What name?'

Soge was thrown. 'What?'

'What name? What name did you ask for?'

Ryan stood level with them looking down into the empty pool at West. 'Don't listen to him, Pauli.'

Mobbs looked back at West. 'I'm wanted in Dublin, you know that. I used a snide passport.'

West looked at him. 'Where does your brother live?'

Mobbs saw a flicker of doubt in his eyes. 'Navan. I'll give you his number; you can call him. He'll tell yer.'

West lit a cigarette. 'He'll tell me what you've told him to tell me.'

Mobbs was at a loss. He appealed to West. 'What is all this, Pauli? You're doin' a number on me like I've put you in the frame.'

Ryan picked up on this. 'You an' that pig's orphan, Venner.'

Mobbs flared. He turned to Ryan. 'Shut your mouth you moron!' He turned back to West. 'It's Venner should be sittin' here, not me.'

West lowered his head and whispered in Mobbs' ear, 'Maybe we can arrange that.'

Mobbs turned his head. 'What.'

West eased back. 'You and me.'

Mobbs was relieved; he could see the beginning of the end of his ordeal. 'How? Jus' tell me.'

'You ring him. Tell him you want a meet.'

There was a strip-search silence. Suddenly Mobbs wasn't so sure. 'But he knows I'm with you.'

West smiled. 'Exactly.'

Mobbs didn't understand. 'How d'yer mean?'

'He'll enjoy turning one of my people.' West considered it for a moment. 'Tell him we've had a falling out, over money. Tell him that. Make it personal. Tell him you want to retire me.'

Mobbs knew this could be dangerous. 'What if he don't buy it?'

'He will,' West assured him. 'We'll make sure of that.'

'How?'

'You offer him a little sweetener.'

'He's a sly bastard. It would have ter be good.'

'Maybe you offer up one of our runs,' West mused, 'one he doesn't know about.' He glanced at Mobbs. 'Maybe your Essex run?' West smiled. 'That's very personal.'

There was a moment of panic in Nicky Mobbs' eyes but he hid it well.

West continued. 'Build it up. Talk some tall figures.'

'That might work.' Mobbs smiled conspiratorially. 'When d'yer want this meet?'

West drew on his cigarette thoughtfully. 'I'll let you know.'

Mobbs relaxed; he thought their business was done with. He tried to move his hands but the wire had cut into his wrists. 'Get me out of this fuckin' thing.'

West made no move to do that. 'So, you up for that, Nicky?'

'You just tell me where and when.'

'Say that again.'

There was something about West's voice, something odd. Mobbs stiffened. 'What?'

'What you just said.'

'What was that?'

West's voice darkened. 'Say it again.'

Mobbs appealed to him. 'Oh, cummon, Pauli. This wire's cuttin' my fuckin' wrists to pieces.'

'I just want to hear you say it again,' West said, as he bent down to stare into Mobbs' face. 'I want to see you say it.'

Mobbs nervously shrugged at the nonsense of it but repeated what he'd said. 'Just tell me where and when.'

West eased back satisfied.

Although it was cold Mobbs had started to sweat.

West pulled on his cigarette. 'You know something, Nicky?' He stepped forward and stabbed the cigarette out on Mobbs' face.

Mobbs roared with pain.

West smiled. 'You've got cat-shit eyes.'

Soge and Ryan dragged a barely-conscious Mobbs out to Ryan's car. Seaman went ahead of them and unlocked the boot. They dumped Mobbs in it, Seaman slammed the lid shut and locked it.

West took the keys from Seaman and tossed them to Jimmy Ryan. 'Lose him.'

Jimmy Ryan unlocked the driver's door. 'Where?'

West was unconcerned. 'Anywhere.'

Ryan opened the door. 'Where are you gonna be?'

West ignored the question. He held his hand out to Seaman. 'I'll take your car.'

Seaman dipped a hand in his pocket, took out his keys and passed them to West, who started to move to the car parked some distance up the street.

Ryan called after him, 'Pauli?'

West stopped and turned.

'How is it you never do none of the shit nowadays?'

West turned back without reply, moved on to the
car, got in, started it and pulled past them down to
the main road.

Seaman was standing away from the car smoking.
Silhouetted by the headlights, Ryan and Soge dragged
Mobbs to the edge of a steep landfill site. They held
him swaying, his feet on the edge of the cliff of waste.
Ryan slipped the gun from his belt, held it to the back
of Mobbs' head and pulled the trigger.

The impact of the bullet pitched Mobbs forward. His
dead body went tumbling down into the darkness.

Ryan wiped a splinter of bone from his face, the
gun held loosely at his side, then he and Soge, without
speaking, turned and made their way slowly back
towards the car.

Seaman flicked his cigarette away and walked across
to them. 'Let's get out of here.'

Ryan looked at him. 'What's the rush?'

Seaman moved to go back to the car. 'Someone
might have heard.'

'What?' Ryan raised the gun. 'This?'

'Put it away, Jimmy,' Seaman said.

Ryan pointed the gun at him. 'You're startin' to
sound like the colonel.'

Seaman gave Ryan a level stare; it was eyes on
eyes.

Ryan grinned, turned the gun from him and emptied
it. The shots tore through the surrounding silence.

Seaman stood looking at him. 'You're fuckin mental.'

Ryan laughed, pushed the empty gun back in his
belt and moved off towards the car.

Twelve

Fran was driving an old car she kept parked well away from the house. She was wearing glasses and a wig she kept hidden in the locked glove compartment. She was a different woman, catching her breath with excitement as she followed the route back into the city. Fran had learned to be more than cautious; she checked the rear view mirror often to make sure that she wasn't being followed.

The antique shop was small, set back from the street, its windows guarded by a metal latticed screen. Fran took a key from her bag, unlocked the door of the flat above the shop and entered.

She closed the door quietly and switched on the light. A narrow staircase with framed boxing prints on the wall lay ahead of her. As she climbed the stairs she slipped the glasses off.

Fran entered the living room, pulling off the wig and shaking her long hair free. She felt for a switch on the wall and turned the light on. The room was warm and comfortable if a little shabby. She dropped the wig and glasses on a chair.

There was a bottle of champagne on the table with two glasses. She smiled and crossed to the table where a note was propped against the bottle. As she picked it up and started to read, arms slipped round her from behind.

'I wasn't sure you'd come.'

She turned to face Mahon, her face suffused with pleasure and a little sadness. 'I can't stay long. Davey might be back tonight.'

He kissed her gently.

Fran loved the touch of his lips, the smell of his body. 'When I saw you at the club I could hardly breathe.'

Mahon was still wearing the tie.

Fran laughed. 'Where did you get that awful tie?'

'It cost me fifty p in a charity shop.'

'You look like a pimp.'

Mahon smiled, took the tie off and dropped it on the table. He picked up the glasses and champagne, kissed her again, then slipped an arm round her shoulder and slowly walked her from the room.

Mahon and Fran lay back in the bed, sharing a comfortable silence after making love. Mahon turned and leant over her. There was a bullet scar in one shoulder, another near the knuckle of his spine. He ran his fingers through her hair and kissed her eyes.

Three months ago Fran wouldn't have believed she could be this happy; at least – when she was with him. She looked at Mahon and smiled. 'It should be like this all the time.' He tried to kiss her silent, but she needed to talk. 'It could be. We could go abroad.' She was caught up in her dream. 'Spain. I love Spain. Andalucia, the white villages.'

Mahon knew the dream was just a dream. 'He'd find us.'

Fran wasn't listening. 'There's a place near Ronda; it's so beautiful.'

Mahon tried to make her face reality. 'He'd find us, Fran.'

Fran reacted. 'He's in prison.'

'If he gets that new trial he could be out in three months.'

Fran could hardly bear to think about the possibility. 'He won't get out; he knows it, his solicitor knows it.'

Mahon knew men like Ray Tolman. They were unforgiving. Their money and connections could buy them anything, including lives. He tried to make Fran accept the situation for what it was. 'Even in prison he's got a long reach.'

Fran moved away from Mahon. 'We can't carry on like this. Sooner or later someone's going to find out.'

He tried to reason with her. 'It's not that simple, Fran.'

'Yes it is. We just go,' she said petulantly.

Mahon wondered why he was so patient with her. 'What about money?' he asked.

'There's money, in a bank account in Malaga. Ray put it there in a joint account in case we had to leave the country.'

Mahon could see that she had it all worked out. 'What about your son? What about Davey? You can't just walk away from him.'

Fran angrily threw back the covers and got out of bed. 'I can walk away from anything and anyone if I knew it was with you.' She crossed to the door, unhooked a robe and put it on. 'Davey doesn't need me.' She turned back to Mahon. 'He never has.'

Mahon sat up in the bed and leaned back against the wall. 'I can't believe that.'

Fran didn't want to talk about her son; didn't want to talk about anything but escape from the life she had grown to loathe. She went back to the bed, sat on it beside Mahon and looked at him with a curious intensity. 'Do you love me?'

Mahon reached out and brushed her cheek with the back of his fingers.

Fran eased away from his touch. Her voiced softened. 'Do you?'

'You need the words?'

'I need the words.'

Mahon spoke as though the air in front of his mouth was fragile. 'I love you, Fran.'

Fran turned, took a cigarette from a packet on a bedside table and lit it. 'You're a strange man.' She lay back on the bed with Mahon. 'There are times when I feel that you're here but not here.'

He knew that what she was saying was true. She deserved some sort of explanation. 'Sometimes I feel . . .' he searched for the right word, 'disconnected.'

Fran didn't know what he meant. 'From me?'

Mahon looked at her. 'From everything.'

Fran could tell from his voice that this was about more than just them; there was something dark and secret in Mahon's life, something he took great care to hide from her.

'I often watch you,' she said, pausing to draw on the cigarette. 'Do you realise how much time you spend staring out of windows?'

Mahon remained reflective.

'I often wonder what you're looking at, what you're

seeing.' She tapped ash into a metal ashtray. 'It's almost as though you enjoy being out of reach.'

Mahon shrugged off his silence. 'It's being in this city, I suppose.' He tried to share some part of his past with her. 'I was brought up on the west coast of Ireland. I don't trust cities.'

In her mind Fran was staring into the bleak reaches of a future without him. 'One day you'll leave, go back to Ireland.' She put her cigarette out and got up from the bed. 'When I think of you I always think of someone walking away.'

Mahon slipped out of bed and wrapped his arms around her. He could feel the warmth of her body through the thin cotton robe. He kissed her gently. 'I'm not walking away.'

Fran reached up and ran the tips of her fingers over his face as though photographing a stranger with her touch. 'I sometimes think I don't know you at all.'

Mahon and Fran were preparing to leave. Fran's growing fear that her son would return to the house, find her not there and start to ask questions, was making her anxious, and yet she was still full of this wrenching love for Mahon and wanted to see him again as soon as possible. She picked the wig and glasses up from the chair and turned to him. 'I'm going to see my sister Wednesday night. I could leave early?'

Mahon looked at her for a moment without speaking, remembering his arrangements with Frankie Pitillo. 'I can't, I'm sorry.'

Fran turned away from him, trying to hide her disappointment.

'I'm sorry, Fran.'

'Sorry.' Fran moved away. 'I hate that word.'

'I've got something on.'

She walked to the door. 'We can't go on like this.'

Mahon moved across to her and slid his arms round her waist. 'It won't always be like this.' He kissed the back of her head. 'We'll work something out.'

Fran moved away from him. 'I could grow to hate you.'

Mahon reached out and gently stroked her neck. 'You don't mean that.'

He was a scatter of contradictions but she could never stay angry with him for long. She turned and took his hand. 'You don't understand. You're the only decent thing that has ever happened to me.' She raised it to her lips and kissed the palm. 'You're the only man who has ever touched me with tenderness.'

Thirteen

Fran saw lights on in the house as she drove past. She continued down the road for some distance, then turned into a side street and parked. She sat in the car, lost in the memory of her brief time with Mahon. She had learned over the months she had known him that pleasure can be its own punishment. She slipped the wig and glasses off and locked them in the glove compartment, along with the keys to the flat, took a brush from her bag and tidied her hair.

As she walked back to the house, she started to build the lie she would tell her son if he was there. The ground floor of the house was in darkness but there were lights on upstairs. Fran called out, 'Davey?' She moved to the stairs, stood at the bottom and called up, 'Davey?' There was no reply. She called again, raising her voice. 'Are you up there?' The silence drew Fran up the stairs. Halfway up she saw spots of blood on the carpet. Her voice filled with alarm. 'Davey!' She started to run up the stairs and saw more blood. As she got to the top she called urgently, 'Davey where are you?'

She followed the trail of blood to a bathroom. As Fran entered she saw Davey, stripped to the waist, bent over the wash basin swabbing blood from a wound in his side with a pad of cotton wool. His bloodstained shirt and jacket lay on the floor. Fran stood in the doorway trying to take it in. 'What happened?'

Davey couldn't stop the flow of blood. He picked up a towel and pressed it to his side. He was deathly pale.

Fran could see that he was close to fainting. She moved towards him. 'Come and sit down.'

She went to touch him but he brushed her away violently. 'Get out!' He clung to the basin to steady himself.

Fran approached him again, more cautiously. This time he allowed her to guide him to the toilet and sit him down on the closed lid. She was trying desperately to stay calm. 'Let me look.'

He still had the towel pressed to his side. Blood had seeped through it between his fingers.

Fran went to move his hand.

Davey's head dropped down onto his knees.

Fran peeled the bloody towel away from his body and saw what looked like a knife wound in the soft flesh under his arm. She went to leave the bathroom. 'I'll get the doctor.'

'No!' Davey snatched his head up and grabbed Fran by the wrist. 'No doctor.'

She tried to reason with him. 'We've got to stop the bleeding.'

He held on to her wrist. 'Let me lie down.' He went to stand. 'I'll be okay if I can lie down.'

Fran helped him to his feet. 'What sort of trouble are you in, Davey?'

He started to move unsteadily towards the door.

'What happened?'

'Someone stabbed me.' He grimaced with pain. 'Ran up behind me and stabbed me.'

Fran found this sort of random, senseless violence impossible to understand. 'Why?'

Davey shook his head. 'I don't know.'

She helped him from the bathroom. 'There must have been a reason.'

'That one don't need a reason; he's a fuckin' crank.'

'You know who it was?'

They made their way slowly down the hallway towards Davey's room. 'I've seen him around; don't know his name.'

Fran opened the bedroom door. 'Does anyone else?'

'Don't you worry,' Davey said. He looked at Fran with the same frightening look that his father had when violent reprisal was on his mind. 'He's got some comin'.'

The lights were dimmed, Davey was sleeping. Fran sat by the bed looking at her son. His fine-boned face, although pale and drawn, was exquisite. Such beauty is wasted in this cesspool city she thought. She recalled the joy of his childhood, and although they had recently become strangers she realised just how much she loved him. Then she remembered what she had said to Mahon earlier. *'He doesn't need me. He never has.'* She leaned forward and gently covered Davey's bare arm with the duvet and thought about Mahon's quiet reply, *'I can't believe that.'*

Of course, he was right.

Fran eased back into her chair and sat locked in a consuming sadness. She felt suspended between the love for her son and her growing love for Mahon. She needed them both but she knew that at some point quite soon she would have to chose between them.

Two hours later Davey woke with a grunt of pain.

Fran stirred; she had fallen into a shallow sleep. She looked at him. 'Are you okay?'

Davey yawned. 'Yeah.'

Fran got up and moved to the bed. 'Let me look.' She pulled back the duvet. There was a stain of dried blood on the sheet. She bent to look at the wound; it was close to the heart. She looked at Davey. 'You could have been killed.'

Davey dismissed it. 'Looks worse than it is.'

Fran pulled the duvet back over him. 'You've got to report this to the police.'

Davey laughed. 'Do what?'

'I'll come with you.'

'They'd be all over me like a rash – Ray Tolman's son stabbed. He had to be up to something, just like his lousy father.' He ran his tongue over dry lips. 'Can you get me a drink?'

'I'm going to tell Ray next visit,' Fran said.

Davey knew his father. 'He'll laugh at you.'

This saddened Fran; she knew it was true. She moved to the door and was about to leave the room when Davey asked the question she'd been hoping he wouldn't.

'Where were you?'

Fran opened the door, avoiding an answer. 'Is tea all right?'

'When I got in you weren't here.'

In the stress of the last few hours she had forgotten her lie; perhaps it had been too elaborate. A new lie was needed. Fran held her back to Davey as her mind raced with a contained fear. 'I couldn't sleep . . . went out for a walk . . . the rain had stopped.'

Davey moved into a more comfortable position. 'Three spoons.'

Fran turned. She was expecting more questions. 'What?'

Davey reached for a cigarette in an open packet on the bedside cupboard, then looked at her. 'Sugar.' He lit the cigarette and eased back in the bed.

As she left the room, Fran realised she was trembling.

Fourteen

It was that elusive time between night and day, just before dawn when the darkness thins. Mahon parked his car close to a small hotel. He was dog-weary but he had one last call to make.

As he entered the hotel Mahon saw that the night porter had his back turned, sorting out keys. He slipped past him and started up the stairs.

He found the room on the third floor and knocked. The door was unlocked and opened. Mahon entered. An older man with a mane of thick hair the colour of an emptied ashtray had his back to Mahon, checking the mini bar. He lifted out a miniature whisky and a glass then turned and handed them to Mahon. He had a fathomless face and sealed eyes as though he was the custodian of some impenetrable secret. 'It sounded urgent.'

Mahon opened the bottle and poured the whisky. 'There's a shipment coming in from Holland.'

James Lynn took out a miniature brandy. 'When?'

'Wednesday night.'

'What is it?'

'High-grade heroin. Nothing big, but it might lead to something.'

Mahon had been seconded from the military police. He was working directly to Lynn, who headed a shadow group made up from customs, drug squad and security operatives.

Mahon was Lynn's secret; none of the group knew about him, only Lynn. He had been undercover for almost a year, buried deep within the criminal community trying to penetrate the city's drug network. Lynn's theory was that if the city was to be reclaimed, it would have to be done by people who were more organised and more ruthless than the criminal drug gangs, who saw the city as theirs.

Lynn had an eerily precise way of speaking. He was a man used to issuing orders and having them obeyed.

Mahon sipped his whisky. 'I'm collecting it.'

'Who for?' Lynn asked.

'Frankie Pitillo. He works with West.'

Lynn opened the bottle and sniffed the brandy. It was undrinkable. He put it aside. 'Where?'

'A motorway restaurant in Essex.'

Lynn's questions were always pared to the bone. 'New connection?'

Mahon shook his head. 'Pitillo said they've been doing it every month for a year.'

'Can you trust him?'

Mahon smiled. 'Frankie Pitillo?'

Lynn qualified his question. 'In this context.'

'If Frankie Pitillo told the truth his teeth would turn black, but I can't see why he would lie about this,' said Mahon.

'What's his relationship with West?'

'As far as I can make out, he gets the stuff collected, checks it, cuts it, bags it into weight and moves it on to the middle men to cut again and push out to the dealers.'

'How close are you to West?' Lynn asked.

Mahon didn't want to overstate it. 'Closer than I was. It isn't easy; he's organised, cautious, hardly uses his home phone – just social calls – doesn't have a mobile, doesn't trust them. He does his business from pay phones.' He sipped the whisky; it warmed him. 'The club gives him a good front and a good income. He can hide drug money. His people are tight; they don't make a move without his say so.'

Lynn listened carefully. 'Have you met him yet?'

'I think I'm going to.'

'Wednesday night?' Lynn surmised.

Mahon shook his head. 'No, he's never around when anything goes down. He's too clever for that; that's what he uses people like Pitillo for. All that Pauli West does is count the money.'

Lynn walked to the window and looked out; dawn light filtered through the buildings opposite. 'It's difficult to know how to play this,' he said, turning back to Mahon. 'I want this Dutch connection but we have to be careful.'

'If there's a sniff of surveillance it's all over – a year's work wasted,' Mahon warned.

Lynn thought it through. 'If they've been doing it all that time they're probably over-confident.' Lynn crossed to the mini bar. 'Just play it straight, exactly as you've been told.'

Mahon knew that he could trust Lynn; he was part priest, part devil, but he could be implicitly trusted when it came to operational intelligence. 'It's coming in on a Dutch coaster. I don't know where it berths, but there can't be too many of them in that area at the same time every month.'

Lynn took out a bottle of whisky and checked the label. 'What about the woman?' This sudden change of subject took Mahon by surprise. 'Has she given you any more?'

It was Lynn who had instigated Mahon's introduction to Fran. He had arranged for them to meet accidentally, but it was supposed to be purely to gather information. The fact that it had developed into an intense and dangerous relationship, Mahon had so far managed to hide from him.

'She knows a lot of drug people through her husband, and she's close to West.' Mahon knew he had to hide his true feelings for Fran from this man. 'I never talk about West to her, but she tells me things about him and her husband. They grew up together; more like brothers.'

Lynn broke the seal on the bottle.

'I only see her occasionally.' Mahon added.

'Do you think West knows?'

'About her and me?'

'These people don't miss much.'

'If West knew, I'd be dead,' Mahon considered. 'She would too, probably.'

Lynn noted the catch in Mahon's voice. 'She's a beautiful woman.' He glanced questioningly at him. 'I hope you're not getting involved?'

Mahon knew how sharp Lynn was; a simple denial would not be enough, it wouldn't convince. He chose his words carefully. 'She was unhappy when I met her. I've used her, made her need me. I haven't liked doing that.'

Lynn poured the whisky.

Mahon hoped he wasn't over-playing the sympathy.

'She's a decent person. She just married the wrong man.'

Lynn sipped the whisky.

Mahon tried to turn it round. 'Do you want me to end it?'

'Is she still useful?'

'She's another hand on West.'

Lynn thought for a moment. 'Did you know her husband has an application for appeal in?'

Mahon nodded. 'She told me.'

Lynn gave Mahon a calculating look and then almost smiled. 'We better make sure he stays where he is then.'

Mahon relaxed. He knew that for the moment they were safe.

Fifteen

Pauli West didn't respect many men; Alan Mercer was one he did. Mercer had been a career criminal for thirty years and had never been arrested. He was a private man, a loner, rarely associated with other criminals, was never seen in the pubs and clubs they frequented. He lived quietly with his family, well away from the city, deep in the Suffolk countryside. Only certain people were allowed to visit his home, and even then not often. Pauli West was one of these. Early on, Mercer had recognised something of himself in Pauli, and through the years Pauli had gone to him for advice and guidance; Mercer had become his mentor. Now Mercer saw him almost as an equal. Almost.

Alan Mercer was one of the wheels in the UK drug network; he had serious drug connections all over the world but he was clever, elusive, almost invisible. Criminal intelligence knew little of him, and certainly didn't see him as a target.

He'd asked Pauli West to drive out to see him. Pauli knew it had to be important. Mercer had a deal going

down with some connected people on the Continent.
It was big, very big. He'd brought Pauli in early but
hadn't so far told him much about it. That's the way
Alan Mercer operated; that's the way he had stayed
so anonymous over the years. No one knew more
than they needed to. It sometimes pissed Pauli off,
but then he knew that in the same circumstances, the
roles reversed, he would do exactly the same.

It was a brisk autumn day with a chill wind that
cut through West's city clothes. Mercer loaned him
a quilted coat and then walked him out into the six
acres the house was set in.

In a paddock some distance from the house, Mercer's
eleven-year-old daughter was riding her pony over
low jumps. Leaning on the fence they stopped to
watch her.

Mercer watched in silence for some time then turned
to West. 'That kid's my life, Pauli.'

West took out his cigarettes. 'She's growing up.' He
measured an eight-year-old with his hand. 'Last time I
saw her she was . . .'

Mercer was troubled. 'She's already asking questions.'

West lit a cigarette. 'She's bound to.'

Mercer's face tightened. 'I don't want her to know
what I am.'

His daughter slowed the pony to a walk and waved
to her father.

He waved back. 'After this one I'm going to retire,
sell up, go somewhere, right away, even abroad
maybe.' Mercer turned and walked away from the
paddock. 'Trouble is it's that voice inside you, that
wrong voice telling you it's always the next score
that's going to be the one, the next deal is going
to be the last; you've just got to take it down!'

West followed on his shoulder. 'This deal is unbelievable, Pauli!'

West looked at him. 'Wrong voice?'

Mercer smiled ruefully. 'Wrong voice.'

West knew Mercer well. He waited patiently until he was ready to say why he'd brought him here. They stood at the boundary of the property looking out over a field being ploughed by two tractors, a flock of screeching gulls hovering in their wake of freshly-turned earth.

'What's this business with Nicky Mobbs?'

West dismissed it. 'That's personal.'

Mercer fixed West with steel-trap eyes. 'There's no such thing as personal now, Pauli. You better start learning that. Anything that affects you affects me. These people don't fuck around; you screw up with them just once and you're gone.'

West pulled on his cigarette. 'Nicky got greedy. He tried to play both sides against the middle. He went to Venner.'

'What is it between you and Venner?'

'Nothing we can't sort out.'

'You better sort it out, Pauli, and fast, or this deal is down the crapper!' Mercer took a tortoiseshell snuff box from his pocket. 'I've told these people we're all set, all sorted, organised.' He opened the box and took a pinch of Spanish. 'I'm going to Brussels next week.' He snorted the snuff then absently ran a finger across both nostrils. 'You come to some accommodation with Venner or you're both out.'

On his way back West had arranged another meet. He was waiting in his car at a motorway service station. He checked his watch. Whoever he was meeting was late. A car pulled in beside him. The driver looked around then got out, locked his car and walked towards the restaurant. West got out and followed a few paces behind.

There was a natural anonymity about these motorway service areas that made them perfect for a meet. They were all the same; the same flashing game machines ambushing the kids as they came in, the same tatty fast food outlets, the same shops selling the same disposable rubbish, the same people dressed in the same clothes driving the same cars. Everything seemed to be transferable, as though it could be scooped up and set down a thousand miles away and no one would notice.

It was mid-morning, a slack period in the restaurant; the travelling salesmen who usually frequented the place were tooling up the motorway listening to their Tina Turner tapes.

Tommy Rook, a tall man in his mid-fifties, settled at a table with a cup of coffee. West soon joined him – they shook hands.

'Sorry I'm late, Pauli.'

'Problems?'

'They're getting busy again. They've had someone following me all week, some moron in a Mondeo.'

'Sounds local?'

'I don't think so.'

'Customs?'

'Could be. I came through Kent, lost him in the lanes.'

West took out his cigarettes. 'Why all this now?'

Rook looked uneasy. 'I don't know. Could just be down to me running an Essex-based haulage company. I mean, anybody with eighteen wheels and a road map is at it over there.'

West couldn't accept this. 'They've been over your vehicles with a flea comb.'

Rook nodded. 'On the Continent, coming in, even in the yard. They're always clean as a cat's arse.'

West tapped ash from his cigarette. 'You've got no form to make them suspect you.'

Rook sipped his coffee. 'Just play it out, I suppose, like last time. They soon get bored.' He pushed on with more immediate business. 'That stuff for Manchester and Newcastle – you still want it shifted?'

'Is it safe to move it?'

'We'll take it in the toxic vans; if anyone stops them they won't be dipping their hands in that stuff.'

Sixteen

Dean, a ten-year-old tearass, made his way cautiously through an inner city estate. Here, people lived on the inside of their skins, violence was the language; you could almost smell the sharp odour of fear. The light hardened as he approached a block and, with a last uneasy glance round, entered. He made his way through the urine-scented passages and ran up the stairs, making his way to the top landing. He never used lifts – they were places of natural ambush. He emerged on to the open landing and made his way to the end. The door of the last flat had a piece of plywood for a window, the paint was peeling, the letter box had been welded up, there was no number. He glanced back to check there was no one else on the landing; although he was only ten he had old and wise eyes. He turned back to the door and knocked. A dog started to bark and a woman's voice came from inside.

'That you Dean?'

Dean hated dogs.

A chain was slipped, two bolts slid back, the door

opened a crack and a young woman peered out. 'Where you bin?' Her face had a wasted beauty.

'You keep that fuckin' dog off me,' the boy said.

She opened the door.

Dean slipped in and flattened himself against the wall to avoid the Alsatian.

Stella had a tight grip on the dog's collar. She bolted and chained the door. 'You're late.' A grubby cotton dressing gown covered her thin body, her nose was running; she wiped it with the back of her hand. 'You got it?'

Dean felt in a pocket, then another.

'Quick!'

Dean took out a wrap of heroin.

Stella snatched it from him then turned and dragged the dog back down the hall.

Dean called after her, 'I can't stay long.'

She dragged the dog into the bedroom and slammed the door.

Dean moved down to the door and called through it, 'Stel, I can't stay long.'

Stella didn't reply; she was already locked into the mystic ritual of the junkie.

The boy moved through the cramped and fetid flat. There were still vestiges left of a normal life having been lived here once. There was a cardboard box of absent-children's toys, a vase of long-dead flowers, a framed print of Robert de Nero in *Cape Fear* hung at an angle on one wall, but the rest was desolation: a few sticks of furniture, a broken television, dusty paper plates of congealed fast food, cigarette tabs everywhere.

He moved into the kitchen. The fridge and cooker had been sold off, the wiring left hanging from the wall. There was a bottle of milk with a scum of mould on top and a half-eaten packet of biscuits. He grabbed a couple and stuffed them in his mouth as he moved to the window and glanced down into the courtyard. He could see a gang of mongrel kids not much older than himself, smoking and fighting, trying to kill time. He made a mental note that they were to be avoided at all costs on his way out. He moved back through the flat to the bedroom and leant against the door. 'I gotta go.' He listened. 'Stel? Come on.'

The door clicked open under his weight.

The dog snarled and bared its teeth but didn't move. A thick piece of foam rubber with a grubby blanket and a caseless pillow served as a bed. The dressing gown was on the floor. Stella, wearing a short T-shirt and pants, had her back to him fixing on the inside of her thigh. She turned to Dean, the empty rig in her hand, flecks of blood left in it. There was a moment of absence in her eyes as the heroin threw its fog upon her brain. She moaned softly, rubbing her thigh, then she laid the rig on a chair, reached for a packet of cigarettes and quickly lit one. Now she was easy. She looked at Dean. 'You want your money?'

Dean was restless. 'Yeah, I gotta go.'

The pants were transparent; he could see her pubic hairs through them, and a folded note.

Stella smiled. 'Better take it then.'

As he moved slowly into the bedroom she moved suggestively towards him. Dean stopped. 'Don't fuck about.'

She pushed her bony body towards him, sticking out her crotch. 'Go on, take it.'

Dean backed away. 'No . . . don't.'

'Don't you want it?' Stella teased.

He reached out slowly to take the folded note from her pants, then drew his hand back.

She laughed. 'Tell yer what. How about a fuck fer the stuff?'

Dean appealed to her. 'I gotta go.'

Stella slowly lowered a hand between her legs. 'You gotta start some time.'

Dean wondered what it would be like, wondered if she meant it, but he was late. 'Davey's waitin' for me.'

She stopped teasing, slipped a hand in her pants, took out the folded note and handed it to him. 'You can tell that Davey I'd fuck him any time fer a free wrap.'

Dean was off, out of the bedroom and down the hallway.

Stella called after him, 'Tomorrow.' She could hear him undoing the door. 'See you tomorrow.'

But he was gone.

The boy clipped down three flights of steps, got to the ground floor and was just about to move into the courtyard when someone slipped from the shadows of a stairwell and grabbed him, dragged him back into the darkness. But the boy was not going to be taken without a fight. He kicked and punched. His attacker was not expecting this and was forced to let go of him. Dean tried to run but slipped and fell. The man was on him again. The boy snatched a knife from his pocket and stabbed him in the knee. The man roared with pain and kicked out at Dean, who tried to stab him again. The man grabbed him. In the struggle the rings the man was wearing on each finger cut the boy's face. He hurled the boy against a wall, knocking him unconscious, then bent over him, searched his pockets and pulled out a fistful of screwed-up notes.

Seventeen

The BMW was parked in a supermarket car park. Davey sat in it smoking and waiting, his face pale and waxy; the stab wound in his side was sore. Smoke curled through the open window as he watched a shapely young sort bend over the boot of her car trying to find space for bulging plastic bags. The girl felt eyes on her; she slammed the boot lid shut and turned to look at Davey. She wasn't expecting to see a good-looking guy in a smart car. She gave him a flirty smile. Davey flicked his cigarette out of the window and was just about to get out to give her a spin when he saw Dean weaving unsteadily between the parked cars. As he got closer Davey could see that his face was marked and his jacket torn. He opened the passenger door and the boy got in. Up close Davey could see the deep scratches the rings had made on Dean's face. 'What the fuck happened to you?'

The boy settled in the seat with angry eyes. 'I was robbed.'

Davey reacted. 'How much?'

'Three hundred.'

'Where?'

The boy's nose started to bleed again; he wiped it on his sleeve. 'I was at Stel's.'

'Them little gangsters from the flats?'

Dean shook his head. 'Nah.'

'Who then?'

The boy turned to him. 'Gotta fag?'

Davey took out his packet of cigarettes. 'Who was it?' He took one out and handed it to Dean. He could see his hands were trembling. 'Did you see who it was?'

'Fuckin' bastard!' Dean stuck the smoke between his swollen lips.

Davey took out his lighter. He was getting angry. 'Are you gonna tell me or what?'

The boy waited for Davey to light his cigarette. 'I've seen him.'

'When?'

'Before.'

'Where?'

'Can't remember.'

'With Stel?'

'Nah.'

'You sure?'

The boy thought again. 'With one of her mates maybe.'

'So she'd know his name?'

'Stel?'

'Wouldn't she?'

The boy shrugged. 'Dunno.'

'So what happened?'

'He was waitin' under the stairs when I come down. I tried to stop him . . .' He indicated the scratches. 'He done this with his rings.' The boy was desperate to be believed. 'I did try, Davey.'

BUY ONE - GET ONE FREE Promotion

Simply tick ONE preferred FREE title, detach this form and send with proof of purchase to: No Exit Press (BGF) , 18 Coleswood Rd, Harpenden, Herts, AL5 1EQ (offer closes 30/9/00 - no photocopies allowed.) Info on the titles can be found at **www.noexit.co.uk**

Name:

Address:

Postcode: e-mail address:

Title of book you purchased:

Free Book Choice:

..... Sunday Macaroni Club/Steve Lopez   ..... Cold Caller/Jason Starr

..... The Last Manly Man/Sparkle Hayter   ..... Box Nine/Jack O'Connell

..... Dead Birds/John Milne   ..... Small Vices/Robert B Parker

..... Perdition USA/Gary Phillips   ..... Under the Bright Lights/Daniel Woodrell

Davey softened. 'I know.' He ran his hand comfortingly over Dean's cropped head. 'I know you did; I can see.'

'Stabbed him in the knee.'

Davey grinned. 'Good boy.'

The boy's breathing suddenly became heavy; his face went grey and pricked with sweat.

Davey looked at him. 'You okay?'

'Feel sick.'

'Not in here!' Davey dived across and snatched open the passenger door.

The boy appeared to recover. 'It's all right.'

'You sure?'

Dean sucked in breath. 'I'm all right.'

Davey checked the boy closely. 'Sure?'

The boy gave him a queasy smile. 'Yeah.'

Davey pulled the door closed then took the cigarette from him and tossed it out of the window.

'What'yer do that for?' Dean protested.

'You shouldn't be smoking; that doesn't help.' Davey started the car. 'I'll drive with the windows open.'

'Where we goin'?'

'Get a bit of air.'

'Where?'

'Let's go and talk to her.'

'Stel?'

'Ask her.'

'What?'

'Find out.'

'What?'

'If she knows him.'

'She won't know.'

Davey looked at the boy. 'Why not?'

'She won't know nothin'.'

'Why not?'

The boy knew her well. 'She'll be out of it by now.'

Davey dropped the car into gear. 'She could be in it with him.'

'Nah.' The boy shook his head firmly.

'Never trust a fuckin' junkie!'

Dean shook his head again. 'Nah, not her.'

Davey reversed out of the parking space.

The boy was sure. 'She's a right Mary; she'd fuck anyone fer a free wrap, but she wouldn't do that.'

Davey wasn't convinced. 'We'll see.'

'She won't say nothin'.'

Davey turned to him. 'She don't co-operate, she gets cut off.'

Dean shrugged. 'She'll jus' go somewhere else.'

Davey changed the subject as he wound the car round the tight bends in the ramp. 'Seen Sammy?'

'He's a div,' the boy said scornfully.

'He's alright.'

'He can't count.'

'He'll be alright.'

'They'll stiff him. You'll be short.'

'Have you seen him?'

'Nah.'

Dean led Davey to the stairwell where the attack took place. 'Here – it was here.' He pointed at the clot of shadow. 'He come from there, grabbed me, dragged me back. I got away but I slipped.' The energy seemed to drop out of his voice as he relived the incident. 'Bashed me against the wall. Head hit the wall.'

Davey took out his cigarettes. 'Big man – kicking the shit out of a ten-year-old.'

Dean took his knife from his pocket. 'I got him in the leg.'

Davey lit two cigarettes and passed Dean one. 'Don't you worry, kid. We'll see how fuckin' big he is.'

Over the dog barking they heard the bolts slide back. The door opened on the chain and Stella peered out with a blank stare; she was having difficulty focusing. 'What'yer want?'

Davey put a hand on the door. 'Not out here.'

Stella looked down at the boy. Even unfocused she could see his face was swollen and marked. 'Christ Dean! What happened?'

Before the boy could answer Davey toed the door. 'Shut that bloody dog up and open the door!'

Stella unchained the door and grabbed the dog by its collar. 'Quiet!' She slapped it hard across its muzzle. 'Be quiet!'

The dog stopped barking but never took its eyes from Davey and the boy as they entered and closed the door.

Close up, Stella could see more clearly the marks against the boy's pale skin. 'Them rotten little swines downstairs?'

Dean shook his head but said nothing.

As they moved down the hallway, Stella pushed the dog in the bedroom and slammed the door shut. It started to bark again and scratch at the door.

The whole flat was airless; stank of the dog and stale cigarette smoke.

Davey moved to the window in the main room. 'Can't you get some air in here?'

Stella watched him for a moment trying to open the window before she spoke. 'The windows are welded.'

Davey turned back to her as though he could not
bring himself to believe what she had said. 'Welded?'

Stella tried to rub some warmth into her thin arms.
'Little fuckers can climb like monkeys.' She turned
away from Davey to the boy, bent down beside him
and spoke softly. 'You all right?'

Dean nodded. 'Feel a bit sick.'

Stella eased her face close to the boy's and looked
carefully at his eyes. 'Headache?'

The boy nodded. 'A bit.'

'How bad?'

'Not much.'

She straightened up and turned to Davey. 'Has he
been sick?'

Davey wasn't expecting this level of concern from
Stella. 'No . . . Well almost.'

She reached out and took the half-smoked cigarette from between Davey fingers. 'He should go to
hospital.'

Dean reacted. 'No!'

'For a check up.'

'I'm alright!'

Stella pulled on Davey's cigarette. 'He could be
concussed.' She passed the cigarette back. 'I did two
years trainin'.' She smiled ruefully. 'Was gonna be
a nurse.'

Dean wanted this right. 'I ain't goin' ter no hospital!'

Davey slipped his cigarettes from a pocket and held
them up to Stella. 'Know a guy who wears rings?'

'Why?'

'He's got money of mine.' Davey pointed to the
boy's face. 'He did this.'

'What sorta rings?'

'Don't fuck me about!'

'I only asked . . .'

'Rings! On each finger!'

Stella turned away. 'No.'

'Who've you told about the boy comin' here?'

Stella stiffened. 'No one.'

'Someone knows when he comes, what he comes here for, what he's carrying.'

Stella looked worried. She knew she could be a bit loose with her mouth. 'They didn't get it from me.'

Davey tossed the cigarettes to her. She caught them, took one quickly from the pack and pushed it between her thin lips.

The boy held up the end of his cigarette for her to light it with. 'I seen him.'

'Who?'

'With that mate of yours.'

Stella passed his cigarette back. 'What mate?'

'With the face. The white face.'

Stella was genuinely confused. 'White face?'

Dean flicked his fingers. 'Black nails.'

'She's not a mate.'

The boy wasn't sure of the name. 'Kath?'

Davey picked up on this. 'Who's Kath?'

Stella half-turned to him. 'She was here once when Dean . . .' It suddenly locked in. 'She knocks about with a nasty bastard.' Now it was starting to make sense to her. 'He wears rings.'

Davey stabbed his cigarette out in a rusting tin lid on the table. 'What's his name?'

Stella thought for a moment. 'Tudge.'

Eighteen

Fran was looking for a light bulb in a cluttered cupboard. As she reached up to a high shelf she knocked down a cardboard box. It fell to the floor and burst open; bundles of neatly faced notes held with elastic bands spilled out. She stood looking down at the money, her face pale and drawn from lack of sleep. She knew it wasn't hers. It wasn't Ray's; he never kept that sort of cash in the house. It had to be Davey's. Scarcely bearable thoughts raced through her mind; where did a seventeen-year-old boy get that sort of money? She bent down, picked up one of the bundles and flicked through the notes. There was nothing less than a twenty. She cast a cold eye over the spill of money and made a rough calculation; there had to be at least ten thousand pounds. Fran recalled how Ray always talked about drug money being 'soft money'. He used to say how easy it was after working the pavement. Armed robbery was a mug's game – the police armed intervention units were kill crazy; even if you weren't shot it was twenty years. Dealing was different; you could make a fortune

out of some other poor bastard's misery. Davey was
the image of his father. He worshipped him. Had he
followed him into the violent and soulless world of
drug dealing? It would explain the stabbing. It was all
starting to fit. Davey was never home. Fran didn't see
him for days at a time, and when she did they rarely
talked. A year ago they discussed most things, now he
was almost unreachable. His old friends were gone. She
didn't know who he was webbed up with now. None of
them came to the house, they wouldn't give their names
on the phone. More often than not, when she answered
they rang off. She bent down and gathered the bundles
of notes – was this Davey's *soft money?* She put them
back in the box. Was it? Oh dear God, was it? She felt
as heavy as death, as though she was watching her life
burn down even further.

Mahon's furnished flat was over a boarded-up pet
shop in an area that had got left behind in the eighties.
It was ordered and clean but small. It hadn't been
decorated for years; the fading wallpaper was a riot
of patterns. The furniture, an old rubbed-raw vel-
veteen three piece suite, was the height of fashion
forty years ago. On one wall were framed photographs of a parachute group; among the red berets
was Mahon dressed in battle camouflage. Close to
them were framed newspaper reports of the Falklands
war.

Mahon was sitting at a table injecting cigarettes with
heroin. He laid the one he had just spiked aside and
picked up one that had dried. He saw that the heroin
had leaked through the paper, staining it. He took the
brush from a bottle of Tipp-Ex and carefully painted
out the stain.

The telephone rang, waking a white bull terrier lying

underneath the table. It looked up and growled. Mahon, annoyed at being disturbed, got up and crossed the room to answer it.

'Hello?'

'I had to talk to you.'

'Where are you?'

'At home.'

'You shouldn't ring me from there, Fran,'

'I know. I'm sorry.'

Fran's voice was thin and strained. Mahon knew something was wrong; she would never take the risk of ringing him from the house unless it was urgent. 'Go for a drive. I'll call you on your mobile.' He rang off abruptly.

Fran sat in her Mercedes, parked in a quiet spot by the river waiting for Mahon's call. Her mobile shrilled, she switched it on. 'John?'

'What's happened?'

'Davey's been stabbed.'

There was a pause. Fran realised that Mahon must have been thinking it was something to do with them; Pauli West finding out about them. She could sense his relief; his voice changed.

'How bad is it?'

'He's all right.'

'Is he in hospital?'

'No.'

'Has he seen a doctor?'

'He wouldn't.'

'Who stabbed him?'

Fran found herself pouring out the whole story: the stabbing, the money, her worst fears. As she listened to herself she realised she was slowly becoming emotionally unravelled.

Mahon listened without interrupting. He knew that Fran just wanted to talk it out.

'I can't go to Pauli – he'd skin Davey if he knew he was turning that stuff. Most of the other people I could ask know Pauli; it would get back to him. Maybe you can find out what he's up to. I've *got* to know.'

'I'm seeing someone tonight.' Mahon was careful not to mention Frankie Pitillo; Fran would make the connection to West. 'I'll talk to him.'

'Would you?' Fran glanced at the river; rowers were out. She could feel tears stinging her eyes. 'I'm sorry, John. There's no one else.'

'I'll ring you tomorrow.' Mahon lowered the receiver then moved to the window and stood looking down into the street. There was a scurf of rubbish on the pavements and in the gutters, left by the market traders.

He watched people passing, seeing only themselves, their problems, as if caught in a maze of mirrors. He sensed that this business with Davey was the beginning of a nightmare for Fran. Her dream of escape to the white villages of Andalucia was gone.

Nineteen

The square mile of congested streets and blind alleys of Soho were always changing; in the fifties the toms and their pimps were on the streets, the punters were robbed and abused, dangerous times. The sixties saw the rise of drugs and the pornocrasy, the working girls moved into grubby rooms up narrow staircases over dirty bookshops and strip clubs. The seventies and eighties came and went with the district losing much of its danger and most of its appeal. At night the no-go areas of Soho were now studded with naf cafes, elite cocktail bars and expensive restaurants where advertising nitwits lived out their consumer fantasies. What had always been a constant in Soho was the bullshit and ego trough of the film industry.

The Porsche was parked outside the office of its owner. He had the traffic warden well-straightened: a fiver a day bought him premier parking bang outside his premises.

Jimmy Ryan and Pete Soge stood looking the

Porsche over. Theirs was more than a passing interest
in customised wheels; this was professional.

The film company offices were on the fourth floor
and the lift was out of order. By the time the two of
them had climbed four flights of stairs they were out
of breath and out of patience. When the receptionist
went to call the police, Jimmy ripped out her phone
and threw it through a window.

The Porsche owner, who had a narcotic promiscuity
that cost him a monkey a week, was holding a board
meeting in his ersatz tinsel town office. On the walls were
framed posters of the films his company had produced;
low budget straight to video exploitation dreck.

Ryan and Soge made a stylish entrance and requested
the keys to the Porsche the finance company had sent
them to repossess.

The Porsche man protested vehemently; coke could
make even a spanner like him feel invincible.

Jimmy Ryan was not a man to be argued with,
certainly not when he was working. He explained to
the Porsche man that one of his favourite films was
Chinatown, and that his favourite scene in it was when
J. J. Gittes got his nose sliced open. He just happened
to have the blade of a knife hovering near the Porsche
man's nose.

The keys hit the table.

Dancer, face like a haddock, no legs, wearing a Crystal
Palace strip, scuffed his wheelchair down the middle of
a busy main road. Drivers wound down their windows
and slagged him as they managed to get past.

The repossessed Porsche slowed alongside him.
Jimmy Ryan leaned out and shouted at him, 'Give
'em a spin, Dancer!' He pulled a handful of notes

from his pocket and tossed them out like confetti.
The money was caught by the wind and distributed
all over the road. Dancer stopped his chair and started
to gather it greedily. Ryan accelerated away choking
with laughter, checking the rear view mirror to see
the chaos he'd caused. Dancer had all but stopped the
traffic in both directions. A car came out of a side road
and cut across the Porsche. Soge braced himself and
shut his eyes. Ryan had to brake hard and swerve to
avoid hitting it. An Arab woman was driving. Ryan
leaned out and screamed at her, 'You bastard foreign
female!'

Soge opened his eyes and looked at Ryan. 'I'd like to
get back with both sides of my body still matching.'

Jimmy grinned; he was enjoying himself. He dropped
a gear and accelerated, drifting the powerful sports car
into a tight right-hand turn off the main road.

Soge nervously lit a cigarette.

They passed a tasty well turned out young blonde
with a bounce in her walk.

Ryan turned to Soge. 'Catch that?'

Soge hadn't noticed her. 'What?'

Ryan slowed the car. 'Walkin' one hip at a time.'
He checked her in the rear view mirror. Soge looked
around. 'Where?'

Ryan pointed. 'That little sex-pest back there.' He
hit the brakes and the Porsche slithered to a stop.

Soge knew exactly what was on Jimmy Ryan's
mind. He appealed to him. 'Oh cummon, Jimmy.
We've gotta get this back and get over to see Pauli
at the club.'

'Pauli can wait,' Ryan snapped, and turned to look
back along the street.

'We're already late,' Soge whined.

Ryan turned back to him. 'Out.'

Soge didn't move.

Ryan leaned across him and opened the passenger door. 'Out!'

Soge knew better than to argue with Ryan when he was in this mood. He got out of the Porsche.

As soon as the door was closed, Ryan crashed into reverse and powered the car backwards at speed, skidding to a stop when he got to the girl.

Soge stood watching Ryan, cocky as a cartoon cat, giving the girl a play. She got into the Porsche.

It pulled away and powered down the road. As it sped past Soge dropped his strides and mooned Ryan.

Twenty

Pauli West and Frankie Pitillo were sitting at a table in the closed bar of the squash club. The bruises on Frankie's face were turning yellow and purple. Against Pitillo's pale, almost transparent skin they looked like a film of petrol on water.

Pauli West didn't have to ask.

Frankie ran his fingertips over his face. 'Someone had a pop at me.'

Something happened in Pauli West's eyes. 'Who?'

Frankie shook his head. 'It all happened so fast. They come out of a shop doorway, whacked me with a bat, threw a blanket over my head and shoved me in a motor.'

Pauli lit two cigarettes. 'Didn't you recognise anyone?'

Frankie shook his head. 'Nah.'

Pauli passed him one of the lit cigarettes.

Frankie pulled on it. 'Probably some pilled-up second division crew out looking to make a name.'

Pauli West considered this. 'How many?'

Frankie tried to work it out. 'Three on me and one driving; four.'

'They got you in the car?'

'The Essex man banged a couple of them, dragged me out – they fucked off.' Frankie could see that he was getting ahead of himself. 'I had this meet with the guy I told you about, for the Essex run, John Mahon.'

'Irish?'

'He's a real find, Pauli.'

'He was with you?'

'We'd just split up. He saw 'em bag me, ran across the road and steamed in. This fuckin' guy had hold of me in the back of the motor, the blanket still over my head. I heard some glass smash then I heard this cunt's jaw go! Crack! Mahon had got hold of the bat and hit him with it, dragged me out.' Frankie grinned. 'He's gonna need a plumber to help him drink a cup of tea!'

'Did he see them?'

'It was too dark.'

'He didn't recognise any of them?'

'The street lamps were fucked.'

West got up and went behind the bar. 'What about Wednesday?'

Frankie turned to him. 'He took some convincing.'

West found a bottle of brandy. 'Cautious?'

Frankie carefully tapped ash into the ashtray. 'He's not like anyone else I know.'

West poured two brandies. 'How do you mean?'

'Quiet. I mean, he hardly says a fuckin' word!'

West carried the drinks back to the table. 'He's a thinker.' He passed Pitillo a brandy. 'What did you offer?'

'A grand or a half off the top.'

'He took the half?'

Pitillo sipped his brandy. 'Wouldn't you?'

'John Mahon you say?'

'He's your sort of person, Pauli.' Frankie tapped his temple. 'Plenty up there and hard as fuckin' nails.'

West sipped his brandy.

West was playing a game of patience and drinking tea when J.W. entered. He looked up. 'Did you get Fran home all right?'

J.W. pulled out a chair. 'We left just after you.'

'How did she seem?'

J.W. sat down. 'A bit blue.' He knew he had to watch what he said. 'I think she's missin' Ray.'

West returned to his cards. 'He'll be out soon.'

J.W. changed the subject. 'What happened with Nicky Mobbs?'

West continued playing patience impassively. 'He's gone.'

A chill ran through J.W.; it was at times like this he realised just how unforgiving Pauli West was.

West checked his watch. 'Where's Dopey and Sleepy?'

'On a snatch back – a new Porsche, for that finance company.'

West looked up at J.W. 'I've just been talkin' to Frankie. Someone had a go at him last night. They came out of a shop doorway, hit him with a bat, slung a blanket over his head, shoved him into a car.'

J.W. lit a cigarette. 'Did he recognise anyone?'

West shook his head.

J.W. played with the cigarette in his slender fingers. 'It could be personal; Frankie's a walking dick. I don't know how he does it with all that shit inside him.' He was used to West not saying much. 'Could be it was some husband and his hangbacks.'

West looked up from the table. His voice had a cool detachment. 'I want to know who it was and what it was about; then we'll deal with it.'

He scooped up the cards and started to lay them out for another game. 'Know anything about a slinger called Mahon? Irish, John Mahon.'

'Yeah, he works the clubs,' J.W. said. 'I know an old black jazzer he looks after, Stumpy Redman.'

West remained impassive. 'I want to know all about him before tonight.'

'Is he doin' the Essex run?'

'Frankie says he's smart and hard.'

'Is Frankie hurt?'

West looked up from the cards. 'He would've been. Mahon smacked a couple of them, pulled him out of the car.'

J.W. was impressed. 'Sounds useful.'

West never took anything at face value. 'Maybe too useful.'

Patience was West's game.

Twenty-One

Stumpy was sat at a table in the club drinking from a half bottle of cooking brandy he'd bought that morning. His cigarette burned into a snake of ash in a cracked glass ashtray full of tabs and the odd roach. The tables round him had the chairs up on them and a big black girl who looked like she could give you a couple of sweaty nights was hoovering the drink-stained carpet and singing softly to herself. Surprisingly, it was Lieder – Schubert's 'Schwestergruss'. She was training to be an opera singer; she was going to be the next Jessye Norman. Stumpy had slept in the band room; he often did when he was out of it. He'd avoided freezing to death by wrapping himself in an old carpet he'd found in a cupboard. Stumpy knew a bit about carpets; he'd hawked them round the suburbs of Chicago once in the fifties, when he was on the blacking. He was almost sure this one was Bokhara. At first he'd thought of smuggling it out of the club and selling it, then he measured what he'd get from some shyster carpet dealer against the life-saving warmth it provided. The carpet remained in the cupboard.

J.W. entered the club and saw Stumpy, who was plainly not aware of anything but the life support in the half of brandy. J.W. made his way across to the girl and slipped her a glove to take the vacuum cleaner and her voice for a coffee. J.W. was a black girl's dream: slim and tall with Harry Belafonte looks. She gave him a smile that promised more than twenty minutes alone with Stumpy, slipped the five down between her breasts and left them to it.

Stumpy became aware of the sudden silence and then J.W. standing there. Fortunately he was only a quarter of the way through the bottle and still coherent. He turned and smiled at the soul man. 'Miles Davis!' He picked up his cigarette. 'Sorry ma man, the gig's gone.' He pulled on the smoke but it had burned down to the tip. 'Try again next week.'

J.W. crossed to the table, lifted a chair down and sat opposite him. 'How y'doin', Stumpy?'

'Scratchin about a bit.' The old tenor man dropped the dead smoke in the ashtray. 'How 'bout you?'

J.W. smiled. 'Lookin' for love.'

'You in last night?' Stumpy enquired.

J.W. shook his head. 'Not last night.'

The old man smiled. 'I was playin' some stuff, swingin' like a rat. Played that old Hawk number – "Bouncin' with Bean" – blew the ass out of it.' He smiled. 'The Hawk would've been proud of me, man.' He paused to lift another cigarette from an open packet on the table. 'I played with him you know, when I was a kid, back in . . .' he tried to cast his muddled mind back, 'fuck it; can't recall nothin'.' Stumpy knew this small talk wouldn't last. He knew that soon J.W. would get around to why he

was there at this time of a rainy morning. 'Man, I tell
you, I felt twenty-five last night.' He lit the cigarette
and exhaled a scarf of smoke. 'Reborn.' Stumpy was
a lush and a junkie but he was no one's fool; he knew
this boy's connection with Pauli West. The old man
wasn't fazed; he'd worked places on the East Coast
owned by people who'd make Pauli West look like a
nun. He waited for J.W. to make his move.

'Seen John Mahon lately?' J.W. asked.

The old man gave a display of deep thought. 'John
Mahon?' He looked at J.W. 'I don't rightly recollect
the name.'

'He's Irish.'

Stumpy knew it wouldn't be too clever to play the
middle eight again. 'You mean Irish?'

J.W. nodded. 'John Mahon.'

'Is that his name?' Stumpy asked.

J.W. moved in. 'What do you know about him?'

The old man smiled. 'He's street.' He settled back
to smoke his cigarette.

'That all?' J.W. asked.

'He sells me good shit; what more do you need to
know about a connection?'

J.W. took out a fold of money with a gold clip on
it. He slid the clip off, peeled a fifty and placed it on
the table.

Stumpy eyed the note.

J.W. put his hand on the fifty. 'I need a bit more
than that, Stumpy.'

'Is he in trouble?' the old man asked.

J.W. shook his head slowly. 'No.' He slid the fifty
across the table.

Stumpy took the money and held it in his hand.
'What you wanna know?'

J.W. shrugged. 'Anything you can tell me.'

Stumpy picked the bottle up from the table. 'He's a quiet man, don't say too much.' He took a drink then looked back at J.W. 'Was in the army. Used to jump from great heights.' He grinned. 'You gotta be cuckoo to do that man.' He looked at the fifty in his hand. 'Listen man, I don't know. He just comes and goes; keeps me supplied, keeps me alive, keeps me playin'.' He pushed the note back across the table. 'I don't have fifty to say about him – I mean, we kick it around, we talk, but he don't say nothin', not about himself. Like I said, he's cool, he's deep; a private man and you have to respect a man's privacy.' He swallowed another mouthful of brandy. 'Tryin' to find out somethin' personal about Irish is like tryin' to pick gnat shit out of pepper.'

J.W. looked at Stumpy, trying to work out if he was telling the truth.

Stumpy shrugged. 'That's it, bro.'

J.W. got up to leave, picked up the note and looked hard at Stumpy. 'If you're lyin' to me, old man . . .'

'Why would I lie? Why would I do that?' Stumpy pointed at the note in J.W.'s hand. 'It's costin' me three bottles of best and change.'

J.W. seemed convinced. 'Who can I talk to that might know?'

'His mother?' Stumpy suggested.

J.W. had to smile at the old man's insolence. He dropped the note back on the table and left without looking back.

As Stumpy watched him go he reached across for the fifty. 'You got no game, nigger.'

Sweets had his back to the door when J.W. entered the bar. He was talking to Charlie Halfway, a big fella with a pink face like a slice of ham who got his street name by never quite getting to where he was supposed to be going. Charlie glanced past Sweets and saw J.W. making his way across the bar towards them. He looked nervously back at Sweets and leant into him. 'You got a date with super-coon?'

Sweets didn't turn. 'You what?'

Charlie pretended not to notice J.W. approaching. 'He's only comin' over.'

J.W. tapped Sweets up from behind.

Sweets spun round and feigned shock. 'Christ! I thought it was the wife!'

J.W. knew Sweets as a clown, but a clever clown. 'A word?'

Sweets' mind was racing what this word might be about, but he hid his apprehension in humour. 'Two if you're buying the drinks.'

J.W. glanced at Charlie. 'Private.'

Whenever any of Pauli West's people were around, it was like a wind blowing through a graveyard; no one quite knew if they were safe. Charlie was relieved to be out of it. He downed what was left of his drink and dumped the pot on the bar. 'I was just off.'

Sweets adjusted his glasses. 'See ya, Charlie.'

Charlie drifted away. 'Yeah, see ya, Sweets.'

Sweets turned back to J.W. 'Haven't seen you around for a while.'

J.W. pointed to Sweets' glass. 'Top up?'

Sweets looked at his empty glass. 'Blue Lagoon.'

This stumped J.W. 'What's that? A cocktail?'

'Cider and meths mixed.'

For a moment Sweets had him. He laughed. 'Dossers' champagne.' He raised his glass. 'No – vodka tonic, thanks.'

J.W bought the drinks and took them over to a quiet corner table and they sat down.

Sweets knew he had to be co-operative but careful; he didn't want a visit from the grievance committee. 'How's Pauli?'

J.W. sipped his scotch and considered the question. 'Pauli is an enigma.'

Sweets stirred his drink with a finger. 'Really?'

'Know what an enigma is?'

Sweets licked his finger. 'Something to make you shit?'

J.W. had to laugh. 'He certainly does that.'

Sweets knew that J.W. was Pauli West's eyes and ears; the brightest of the wild bunch, the least violent. If it had been Jimmy Ryan sitting opposite him he wouldn't have be feeling too secure; mad Jimmy was sent when Pauli wanted to rain on people. J.W. was usually sent on fact-finding missions. He would politely but firmly extract information. But Sweets knew that facts can be funny things; they mean different things to different people.

J.W. came to the point. 'You know John Mahon?'

This took Sweets by surprise. He didn't answer.

J.W. pushed. 'I hear you know him.'

Sweets wondered what the big Irishman had been up to. 'Yeah.'

'You two are close?'

Sweets took comfort in the fact that he was a fluent liar. 'Yeah.'

'I was just talking to Stumpy about him.'

Sweets looked puzzled. 'Stumpy?'

'Stumpy Redman?'

Sweets shook his head.

'Old black jazzer. Your man looks after him.'

Sweets shook his head again as if everything about John Mahon was a mystery to him. 'I don't know nothin' about that.'

J.W. smiled reassuringly, took out his cigarettes and lighter. 'There's no problem, man.' He opened the packet and offered Sweets a cigarette. 'Pauli's looking to put something his way. Asked me to check him out.' J.W. shrugged innocently. 'That's all.'

Sweets eased and took a cigarette. 'He's his own man.'

J.W. held the lighter across the table.

'You can't put the hand on him.'

J.W. lit Sweets' smoke. 'That's what Stumpy said.'

'Very Irish.'

'Ex army?'

'That's right.'

'Parachute regiment?'

'Right.'

'Mad fuckers!'

Sweets thought it wouldn't hurt to let Pauli West know who he was dealing with. 'You should see him on the malice.'

J.W. lit his own cigarette. 'Mahon?'

Sweets sucked in his breath. 'Serious!'

Stumpy was sat at a window table in a Soho cafe with a cup of coffee and a cigarette. A sour looking woman with a mouth like a chicken's arse was behind the counter cutting sandwiches for the lunchtime office rush.

Mahon entered. He knew it had to be important for Stumpy to be out and about at this time. He pulled out a chair and sat. 'What's up?'

Stumpy pulled on his cigarette. 'Wanna coffee?'

'No thanks.' Mahon tried to move the old man along. 'You in trouble?'

Stumpy became serious. 'No, but I think you might be.'

Mahon took this in but said nothing.

Stumpy leaned forward. 'Had some hamster in. Came to the club this mornin'.'

Mahon had to smile at Stumpy's Brooklyn slang for a black.

Ultra cool type, thinks he's Miles Davis.' Stumpy wheezed a laugh. 'Fuck – you blacker than he is. Called J.W. You know him?'

'Of him. He works for Pauli West.'

'That man is bad to the bone. You don't want no shit with him.'

Mahon thought about it. 'What did he want?'

'Everything about you that I know.'

'What did you tell him?'

'Everything about you that I know.' Stumpy grinned showing a gold tooth. 'Which is precisely nothin'.'

Mahon smiled. 'Thanks Stumpy.' He took some cash from a pocket and tried to reassure the old man. 'It's okay.'

'It ain't okay.' Stumpy was offended. 'I don't want your money. You're good folk. I like you, Irish. I want you to stay well, understand? You're my medicine man.'

Mahon put the money away and prepared to leave.

'Stay away from the bad guys.' Stumpy looked sternly at Mahon. 'You hear me?'

Mahon moved to the door. 'I hear you.'

Stumpy watched him pass the window and make his way down the street. The old man's face was full of concern for the big Irishman.

The club was filling up with the squeaky plimsolls and black-eye brigade. A noisy game of squash was being played on the court below the bar.

Pauli West was sat at the end of the bar with a cup of

coffee. J.W. entered and joined him. 'What you got?' West asked.

'I talked to Stumpy and a face called Sweets, couple of other people who know Mahon. He sounds quite a handful.'

'Is that so?' West said flatly.

J.W. glanced briefly around him to make sure they wouldn't be overheard, then turned back to West. 'He was in the army, parachute regiment. Half-killed a guy in a pub, civilian, broke his hands on him so he started biting chunks out of him.'

This appeared to amuse West.

'Did three years in a military prison, dishonourable discharge. He drifted down here about a year or so ago, started selling rolling tobacco on the lazy trade round the pubs and car boot sales. Then one of his suppliers offered him some stuff he had to turn. That's what he's been doin' ever since. Built up a nice little trade; regulars, they seem to trust him.' A young girl came to the bar to get change for the fruit machine. J.W. glanced at her and waited until she was gone before he continued. 'No one's got a hand on him. He's a loner; makes money, lives light, got a rented flat over a pet shop, drives a ten-year-old car.' He lit a cigarette. 'He sounds ambitious, Pauli.'

'He does, doesn't he,' said West. He looked away and thought it through, then turned back to J.W. 'Give Frankie a call. Tell him it's on.'

Twenty-Two

The pub was old and shabby. The barmaid had a thin bony face that was made to look more severe by her hair, which was scraped back and jailed in a bun. She stood at the end of the bar, bored out of her skull, painting her nails a lurid pink.

Three men sat at a table drinking; they'd been drinking most of the afternoon. One of them was a big man but he was out of condition. He had a wall eye and long greasy hair. On each finger of both hands he wore a silver ring. He finished his pint with a swilling gulp then stood up and extravagantly pulled out a fist of money. 'Get 'em in.' He thumbed a note off and dropped it on the table, then limped off towards the toilet stuffing the money back in his pocket.

Every move he made had been observed from another bar.

The toilet was evil: the walls were painted black, the stalls were cracked and stained, there were pools of piss and wet paper on the floor. Tudge entered, unzipped and stood unsteadily in one of the stalls, hosing and farting.

'Nasty limp.'

The voice turned Tudge.

Davey smiled. 'Hurt your leg?'

Tudge was surprised; he hadn't heard Davey enter. He shook his dick and zipped up. 'What the fuck's that got to do with you, smiler?'

The smile decayed on Davey's face. A second kid, built like a tanker, stepped up behind him.

Tudge stiffened. 'What is all this?'

The kid moved with amazing speed for someone so big. He cracked Tudge in the mouth, who went flying back against the wall, blood oozing from his lips and loosened teeth.

Davey stepped towards him. 'All this . . .' he butted his head forward like a ballpeen hammer, splitting Tudge's nose open, 'is about a little ten-year-old scrap of a kid you kicked unconscious.'

Davey's pal hit Tudge again; you could hear his jaw crack in the bar.

The demolition of Tudge was over; he slid down the wall, his face like a pizza.

Davey bent down and searched him for the stolen money. Some of the notes fell on the floor as Davey pulled them from his pocket. As he gathered them he watched Tudge on all fours crawling through a pool of piss towards the wash basin to pull himself up.

Davey let him get slowly to his feet then kicked him in the knee where Dean had stabbed him.

Tudge crashed to the floor, clutching his knee in agony.

Davey pulled a gun from inside his jacket, stood over Tudge and punched it down at him. 'You ever go near him again, you festering pig, I'll kill you.'

He put the gun back in his jacket pocket and they left.

They crossed the saloon bar not even glancing at the two men waiting for Tudge to return.

Twenty-Three

It was foul weather; wind against rain. The estuary waves were capped with white spray. A young Dutch seaman wearing a quilted jacket left a coaster berthed at a private quay used mainly by dredgers. His hands were punched into his pockets, his head down as he battled against the wind along the quay. The rain stung like gravel thrown in his face and the legs of his trousers flapped like flags.

At the gate a girl was waiting in a parked car. When she saw him approaching she started the car and switched the lights on. He got in and kissed her, then she dropped the car into gear and drove away.

Rain lashed the motorway restaurant. Mahon was sitting alone at a window table, absently stirring a cup of coffee and looking out at the parking area. He was wearing an identical quilted jacket. He saw the car pull in and stop. He checked the registration against a number scribbled on a scrap of paper he was holding, then he saw the Dutchman get out, have a parting word with the girl and walk to the restaurant entrance. Mahon checked his watch; his contact was on the dot. He screwed up the scrap of paper, dropped it on the floor and got up from the table.

In the restaurant toilet the Dutchman was sluicing his face at a wash basin, his jacket hung on one of the pegs provided.

Mahon entered but ignored him when he saw a father trying to get his four-year-old son to piss straight. He moved to a cubicle and opened the door. Once inside Mahon bolted the door, took the jacket off and waited.

The father soon left with his child.

When the Dutchman was sure they were gone he moved to the cubicle and tapped lightly on the door.

The bolt clicked back, the door opened and Mahon stepped out. He passed his jacket to the Dutchman, who started to pull it on. He had done this a dozen times before; he could have done it in his sleep. It was Mahon's first time. He wanted to get it right; a year of dangerous undercover work could depend on it. They both kept a wary eye on the door in case someone came in. Mahon moved to the peg and lifted down the other jacket. It was heavy. He weighed it in his hand and turned to the Dutchman. 'Feels about right.' The Dutchman dipped his hand into the pocket of the jacket they had exchanged and took out a tight roll of notes held with a rubber band. He smiled at Mahon. 'Looks about right.' He dropped the money into a pocket. 'Where's Nicky?'

Mahon was putting the jacket on. The question surprised him. 'He's sick.'

The Dutchman was genuinely concerned. 'Nothing serious?'

Mahon zipped the jacket up and shrugged. 'I don't know.'

'Tell him I see him next month, eh?' Then surprisingly he offered his hand. Mahon shook it. The Dutchman turned and left.

Mahon waited a few moments then followed the Dutchman out.

It was all so breathtakingly simple. Mahon almost admired whoever had devised it; probably Pauli West.

A small video monitor attached to an infrared camera hidden in a van parked close to the restaurant showed a degraded image of the entrance and part of the car park. On it Lynn watched their mark leave the restaurant. The girl drove up to the entrance, collected him and accelerated away. He checked the video recorder and turned back to the monitor as Mahon was leaving. He watched him cross to his car and drive off in the opposite direction.

Mahon drove back along the motorway. Heavy lorries churned past sending up blinding veils of water. He was in no hurry; he had plenty of time to get to his meet with Frankie Pitillo. He thought of how he would approach him about Davey. He would have to be careful; Frankie was as sharp as a shithouse rat. It would be fatal for him to make any connection, however small, between him and Davey's mother. He knew he would have to chose his moment. Maybe there wouldn't be a moment, maybe he wouldn't get an opportunity at all. Frankie Pitillo knew everyone in the drug hierarchy from the DDs to the bad-hats who wound the clock. If Davey was at it he would know.

The swelling on Frankie Pitillo's face had gone down but it was still badly bruised. One of his hands was bandaged. He was sitting at a small table carefully cutting the jacket open with a pair of scissors. Sewn into the quilted padding were small sachets of pharmaceutical heroin. He looked up at Mahon. 'No probs?'

'The coffee was like horse sweat,' Mahon said laconically.

Pitillo laughed. 'Listen big fella, the gig's yours if you want it. Every month on the month.' As he cut them out he laid the sachets of heroin in a neat line. 'No aggravation; it's a lovely little tuck.'

'This was a one off, Frankie,' Mahon reminded him. 'Your man was sick.'

The jacket was in shreds. Frankie extracted the last sachet from it and laid it with the others, then he looked up at Mahon again. 'He's gone.'

Mahon sensed that the way Frankie used the word *gone* didn't auger too well for his predecessor. 'I've got my own thing going.'

Pitillo leaned back in his chair. 'Am I hearin' what I think I'm hearin'?' He eyed Mahon with disbelief. 'You turnin' down money?'

Mahon shrugged. 'Money can be its own quarrel.'

Frankie dismissed this. 'That's too fuckin' deep for me.' He studied Mahon for a moment. 'What do you make in a week?' He leant forward. 'One – one an'a half tops?'

Mahon didn't contest the figures.

'With this you get a week's wages fer two hours work. Fer doin' fuck all; a drive in the country and a lousy cup of coffee.' Mahon let him talk. 'How many cluckers do you have to feed to make that sort of money?' He looked for a reaction but Mahon remained impassive. 'You go schleppin' round looking after these people and they don't give a dog's dick about you. They'd sell you to get well.'

Mahon was stirred to reply. 'You're wrong.'

'Am I?'

'You're wrong about most things, Frankie.'

This pissed Pitillo. He knew everything there was to know about the whacked-out world of addiction. 'Listen man, I wrote the fuckin' book. I've done more shit than your lot put together. My body's like a second-hand dart board. I know how junkies think; they don't think . . . that is about anything but gettin' a works in their hand and stickin' that spike in some part of their anatomy.' His anger spilled over. 'You think you're safe? In your fuckin' dreams! It takes just one of them to be pulled for possession. Eight hours in a fuckin' cell an' they're gonna feel like raw meat; they're gonna offer up anyone to get well.' He jabbed a nicotine-coated finger at Mahon. 'And guess what the first name is that comes into their shitty little minds?'

They were in the storage room of a dry cleaners. There was a broken steam press waiting to be repaired, drums of dry-cleaning chemicals and racks of clothes cocooned in polythene.

Mahon looked around. 'Is there a jacket here I can have?'

But Frankie wasn't finished with him. 'The drug boys would just love you. They hate micks, they almost hate micks as much as they hate cannibals. They'd bury you.'

Mahon got up and started sorting through a rack of dry-cleaned jackets waiting to be collected.

Frankie turned to him. 'You work for Pauli, you get protection. He's got half the fuckin' Drug Squad straightened.'

Mahon found one he thought would fit. It was heavy cloth with suede trims on the shoulders. He lifted it down from the rail and started to strip the polythene from it.

'If it wasn't fer Pauli my feet wouldn't touch,' Pitillo continued. 'I could be lookin' at a ten.'

Mahon pulled the jacket on. It fitted perfectly. He checked himself in a wall mirror. 'This'll do.'

Frankie despaired of the big Irishman. 'You're not fuckin' listening, are you?' He made a last effort to make Mahon see sense. 'Do the Essex run fer a while. It could lead ter somethin'.'

Mahon buttoned the jacket. 'I like it on my own.'

Pitillo gave up and turned back to the table. 'I'll cut your half out later, okay?'

'When can I pick it up?'

Frankie checked his watch. 'Say . . . eleven.'

Mahon left the shop and walked down the street. It had stopped raining, the air was fresh; Mahon breathed in deep. Behind him a parked black cab pulled out; its lights switched on as it accelerated and stopped alongside him. The driver lowered his window. 'You call a cab?'

Mahon stopped and turned. 'No.'

The cabbie had the demeanour of a drummer monkey: he was wound up and he wanted to go. 'Yes yer did. Get in.'

Mahon understood. He opened the passenger door and climbed in the back.

The cab clattered through the city heading towards the river. The driver was silent. Mahon sensed that this was what he had been working in deep cover for nearly a year for: to get to Pauli West. He knew that he had to be at his best; West was a clever and dangerous man.

For a moment Mahon felt nervous, but only for a moment.

Twenty-Four

The taxi pulled up in a dark side street on the south bank of the river. The driver pointed to an old tea warehouse that was being converted. 'Through that door and up the stairs to the top.'

Mahon got out. As soon as he shut the door the cab pulled away and drove off into the darkness. Mahon walked to the door, opened it and entered. A long flight of wide stone stairs faced Mahon. He started to climb them.

The top floor of the warehouse was a gothic space full of shadows; the dividing walls had been ripped out and the ceiling supported with metal props, the floor was crudely laid concrete, stacks of bricks, bags of plaster and piles of timber lay everywhere. Bright moonlight filtered through high windows giving everything a ghost-like appearance. West stood at one of the windows looking out at the river like a grey scar on the face of the city. A brightly-lit pleasure boat with a party on board went gliding past, faint music hung in the still night air.

Mahon entered, a touch out of breath.

West turned to him. 'Quite a climb.' Mahon's heels clacked on the cold concrete as he walked towards him. 'They haven't got the lifts in yet.' He gestured proudly round the empty space. 'What do you think?'

Mahon stopped and stood off.

'It's going to be a restaurant. Top drawer, nothing but the best.' West turned back to the window. 'Look at that view.' Across the river Mahon could see the great dome of St Pauls and all round it, in a million shades of grey, the heart of the city. West turned back to Mahon. 'History wherever you look.'

Mahon took in the panorama. His voice was flat. 'Very nice.'

West stepped away from the window and approached Mahon. 'You're not impressed?'

'I don't like cities.'

'Why is that?'

Mahon shrugged. 'They're soulless.'

West smiled. 'Country boy?'

For a moment Mahon seemed to slip into his past. 'A long time ago.'

'Where?'

'You wouldn't know.'

'Try me.'

'Oranmore.'

'Near Galway?'

Mahon was surprised that West knew this.

'My mother was Irish,' West infomed him. 'Finglas, just outside Dublin.'

'What do you want?' Mahon asked abruptly.

West was surprised at his directness; it bordered on bad manners. 'Frankie's been telling me good things about you.'

Mahon didn't appear that interested. 'Has he?'

'How did it go tonight?'

'Hasn't Frankie told you?' Mahon asked, suspecting that Pitillo had known all along about this meeting with West and had phoned to report their conversation at the shop. He gestured to a telephone on the wall. 'I notice the phones are in.'

West smiled. He knew from Mahon's first words that he was a cut above the men who worked for him. 'He said you're our man.'

'Tonight was a one-off, that was the deal. I told Frankie that. Your man was sick.'

'That's right,' West said, then added. 'He died.'

The way West said this made Mahon's scalp crawl. In the moonlight West's pale-green eyes looked almost transparent, like fish scales. Mahon knew he was in the presence of an evil man, but even so there was a degenerate grace about Pauli West.

'I'm doing okay by myself,' Mahon said, repeating what he had told Frankie Pitillo.

West smiled. 'You don't call that money do you? That's nothing.'

'It might be nothing, but it's my nothing,' Mahon replied.

West lit a cigarette. 'I thought you was an ambitious man?'

'That depends.'

'On what?'

'Staying out of prison.'

'Only foolish men go to prison,' West observed. 'The skull busters, the morons who work the pavement. People who don't think.' He paused. 'I've got you down as a thinking man.'

Mahon knew he had to be careful how he played this game. 'Two years, tuck the money away, then I'm back to Ireland.'

'To sit in the sun?'

Mahon ignored the sarcasm. 'Do a bit of fishing. Have you ever fished?'

West shook his head. 'No, I never have.'

'It takes a lot of patience to fish,' said Mahon, turning it back on West. 'I've got you down as a patient man.'

West's smile never reached his eyes. 'Two years?'

'Maybe three.'

'Going to make enough?'

'How much do you need?' asked Mahon.

'Depends on how you like to live.'

Mahon let this slide by.

West dropped the half-smoked cigarette and smeared it out with a foot. 'Well . . . if you want to rot in Ireland . . .' He checked his watch. 'I've got an appointment with my accountant.' He moved off as though Mahon had been summarily dismissed.

'What's on offer?' Mahon asked.

West stopped and turned but didn't answer.

Mahon knew that this was the moment. He hoped he hadn't over-played the reluctance. 'Just curious.'

West took a few steps back towards Mahon. 'Things are changing, getting organised. A drug network is developing all over Europe; some powerful people are involved.' He took out a packet of cigarettes. 'I'm going to need different people, thinking people, people with vision.' He saw the packet was empty and tossed it away. 'Think about it.'

West walked briskly away from Mahon.

Mahon called after him, 'How do I get in touch with you?'

West threw his reply over his shoulder. 'Through Frankie.'

A door slammed and he was gone.

Mahon walked slowly to a window and looked down at a tug towing two barges of waste punching its way down the river.

So that was Pauli West, he thought. He turned and made his way back across the echoing space to the door he had entered by.

Twenty-Five

In the taxi back to the dry cleaners, Mahon's thoughts were not about West but with Fran. How would he broach the subject of her son with Pitillo without raising suspicion? He knew that Fran would be waiting for his call in the morning. She would expect something from him. All of her married life since she was seventeen she had expected things to be done for her and the men around Ray Tolman made sure they were done. Fran had been protected from the more trying realities of life. What she expected she usually got. There was an edge of this in their relationship; it was the one thing about her that angered him. Mahon knew that Fran would take his call in the morning, sitting in her thirty-thousand-pound Mercedes, and she would expect a result. As the taxi wound round the littered streets of south London, Mahon wondered if it was possible to love a woman without judging her.

Frankie was smoking, lounging back in a chair with his

feet up on the table. The heroin had been checked, weighed, cut, bagged and collected. Frankie saw it as his duty to have a little taste; he was loose.

Mahon was with him.

'Here . . .' Frankie said, taking one of sachets from his pocket. 'You did great.' He tossed it to Mahon.

Mahon was only expecting a half; this must have been at least an ounce. He looked at Frankie and could see he was wired. 'Were you straight when you weighed this?'

Pitillo smiled showing his decayed teeth. 'Call it a bonus.'

Mahon tossed it back to him. It dropped in his lap. 'I'll take the half.'

Pitillo almost fell off the chair. 'You must be fuckin' mental.' He snatched the sachet up. 'That's double bubble.'

Mahon wasn't interested. 'I did a job for a price.'

Pitillo was never sure when Mahon was joking. 'Are you serious?'

'A half, Frankie,' Mahon said quietly.

Pitillo took his feet from the table and stabbed out his cigarette. 'Pauli rang me, told me to . . .'

Mahon's voice tightened. 'Do it.'

Pitillo got up and went to a holdall on a chair. 'You're fuckin' weird.' He unzipped the holdall and lifted out a set of sophisticated digital scales, then turned back to Mahon. 'A real hard head.'

'I'm my own man, Frankie,' Mahon said.

Pitillo placed the scales on the table, switched them on and checked the zero reading. Then he opened the sachet and started pouring heroin into the pan. He glanced up at Mahon standing watching him. 'Don't get on the wrong side of Pauli. He can be very . . .' he searched for an appropriate word, 'awkward.'

Mahon saw his chance as Pitillo weighed off a perfect half. 'Do you know a young dealer called Davey?'

Pitillo, only half listening, checked the digital read out. 'Sixteen-seventeen.' He glanced up from the scales. 'Davey who?'

Mahon shook his head. 'I don't know.'

Pitillo emptied the half into a pinch-seal bag.

Mahon was guessing. 'Works the kids at the clubs.'

Pitillo pinched the seal closed and held the half out to Mahon. 'What you wanna know for?'

Mahon knew Frankie would ask this. 'He sold some bad stuff to one of my people.'

Frankie shook his head. 'Sorry.'

Mahon took the bag. 'She said he looked like he was just out of school.'

Frankie grinned. 'Little fuckers. They're gettin' younger all the time. Next thing we'll have eight-year-olds at it.'

Mahon knew he could only push so far. 'Tall, dark, she said he looked like a young Tom Cruise.'

Frankie lit a cigarette. 'Every fuckin' dealer looks like Tom Cruise when you're lookin' ter score.' He grinned. 'Even me.'

Mahon sensed he would get nothing from Pitillo; whether he knew nothing was a different matter. He turned to leave.

Frankie stepped forward and caught Mahon by the arm. 'Pauli's dead set on you workin' for him.'

Mahon didn't like to be touched. He eased Frankie's hand from his sleeve. 'I'll think about it.' He made his way to the door, unlocked it and looked back.

Pitillo was lighting another cigarette. He looked up at Mahon. 'You do that.'

Twenty-Six

'I rang you – rang and rang.'

Mahon dropped down on a seat next to Sweets in the late night drinking club.

'You look hammered,' Sweets observed.

The meeting with West had drained Mahon; he would sleep like the dead.

Sweets glanced round at the faces in the club, suspicion was second nature to him, then he turned to Mahon and lowered his voice almost to a whisper. 'What is this between you and Pauli West?'

The words floated in the dead air between them. Mahon felt a sudden unease at the way the question was put.

Sweets pushed. 'What are you up to?'

Mahon had learned to trust silence.

Sweets dragged his chair closer. 'He's bin makin' enquiries.'

The tinny light in the club gave the drink-addled faces an eerie mask-like appearance. Mahon looked at Sweets. 'I know.'

'He sent Mr Black to talk to me.'

'Stumpy too,' Mahon said.

Sweets pushed his glass of whisky closer to Mahon. 'He give me some old fanny about Pauli puttin' somethin' your way. Is that right?'

Mahon didn't answer.

'I wouldn't trust a word that black cunt said.' A thought suddenly occurred to Sweets. 'You bin eatin' off Pauli's plate?'

Mahon shook his head slowly.

Sweets was not convinced. 'Cos if you have you're bang in bother, boy.'

Mahon picked up the glass and took a swallow.

'That Pauli West pisses charm,' Sweets said, with just a hint of irony. 'You mess with him and he's gonna break about a yard of your back.'

'There's no problem,' Mahon said quietly.

'You sure?'

'Sure.'

'You wouldn' Jack me?'

Mahon pushed the glass back to him and smiled. 'Would I even try?'

Sweets picked up the glass and fierced the whisky down. He raised the empty glass. 'Want one?'

Mahon shook his head.

Sweets caught the barman's eye and ordered another drink with hand signals, then turned back to Mahon. 'So what's it all about?'

In another part of the club a drunken stream of picturesque abuse rose above the general buzz of conversation.

Sweets looked across. 'I see we've got royalty in ternight.'

Mahon changed his mind. He turned and called to the barman, 'Frank.' The barman turned to him. 'Make that two.'

Sweets could read Mahon better than anyone. 'You don't wanna talk about it, do yer?'

Mahon turned back to him. 'There's nothing to talk about.'

Sweets knew that getting anything out of Mahon was like trying to eat soup with a corkscrew.

The barman brought their drinks across. Sweets looked up at him. 'Slate it, Frank.'

The barman picked up the empty glass from the table and moved morosely away. 'Dunno about a slate. You need a fuckin' blackboard.'

Mahon glanced around the club at the faces with their magpie eyes sitting drinking and discussing crime as the night burned away. Sweets was raised in a criminal family; he'd been thieving since he was four. This was the only world that had any meaning for him. He fixed Mahon with a level stare. 'Let's have it.'

Mahon picked up his glass of whisky. 'What?'

'Something's up.'

Mahon sipped his whisky. He knew that Sweets could be trusted. 'What do you know about Davey Tolman?'

Sweets looked at him for some time without speaking, his eyes remote behind glasses, then he moved closer. 'I know his father is not a likeable man.'

'I'm not asking about his father.'

'What are you askin'?'

'Is the kid dealing?'

'Penny bags of sherbet, small stuff. He works the estates. Has these kids, real kids, ten, eleven, turnin' it for him.' Sweets picked up his glass and swilled his whisky round. 'He's a tough little monkey,' he took a drink, 'and spiteful with it.'

'Who supplies him?' Mahon asked.

'That fuckin' hump Frankie Pitillo.'

This somehow didn't surprise Mahon. 'That figures.'

Sweets eased away. 'That's all I know.'

'That's enough,' Mahon said.

Sweets could smell trouble. 'Now you listen to me. You don't know this city like I do. Pauli West and Ray Tolman can turn your piss black jus' lookin' at you. They're evil people. Stay away from that kid; he's fuckin' poison!'

Twenty-Seven

A group of predatory young businessmen emerged from a dinner party at an exclusive restaurant in private grounds. The men wore black tie, the women haute couture. They stood around talking, waiting for their cars to be brought round. David Leahman, a high-flying city accountant, made a show of tipping the doorman. The first car round was a new Ferrari. The valet got out and left the motor running, the driver's door open. Earning his tip, the doorman opened the passenger door. Leahman and his girlfriend said goodnight to the others, got in and drove off with a whimper of tyres.

The Ferrari powered through the city weaving from lane to lane through the thinning night traffic. The girl glanced at Leahman. He was driving too fast but she said nothing. It pulled up at the entrance to a post-modern apartment block. Leahman, his tie hanging undone, shirt collar open, kissed the girl. She could taste the ten-year-old whisky on his tongue.

He slid her dress up and slipped his hand between

her thighs. She knew what it meant. 'You're not coming in?'

'Not tonight. I've got an early morning meeting.'

She delicately removed his hand and straightened her dress. 'Be careful driving back; you've drunk too much.'

Leahman took out a small gift-wrapped box from his pocket. 'You can thank me properly tomorrow night.'

The girl took the present and opened it. Inside a small leather box were a pair of sapphire earrings. She smiled at Leahman, kissed him, then unzipped his trousers and slipped her hand inside.

An electronically operated door whined to a tilt. The Ferrari's headlights bayoneted into the garage and flared on a wall as the door closed. Leahman got out and went to a switch on a wall. He clicked it up and down irritably; the garage light wasn't working. A spill of light from the house filtered into the garage.

A voice from the shadows startled him. 'Nice car.'

Leahman whirled round.

'New?'

Leahman could just make out three silhouetted figures standing in the semi darkness. He tensed. 'Pauli?'

West's voice was clipped and cold. 'Where's my money?'

Jimmy Ryan and J.W. emerged from the darkness.

Leahman's heart thumped in his throat. 'Your money's invested, Pauli. I explained.' He backed away from the two men. 'I've got copies of the papers in the house.' He went to move towards the door that led into the house. 'Come in, have a drink. I'll show you.'

Ryan and J.W. grabbed Leahman, stuffed a rag in his mouth and dragged him back to the Ferrari. One of his hands was forced down and held on the blood-red bonnet.

He was petrified.

West stepped from the shadows. 'You've got a greasy thumb you fuckin' sheeny.'

J.W. spread Leahman's fingers then Ryan slipped a small axe from inside his jacket and brought the blade down severing the thumb.

Twenty-Eight

It was the perfect day for playing golf: a brochure-blue autumn sky and no wind. Most of the members were out on the course, a few old buffers clung to the bar in the clubhouse.

A small figure wearing a hooded anorak that concealed his identity slipped into the bar and up to a wall. He took something from inside the anorak and started to tap at the wall.

The noise turned the people at the bar; they hadn't noticed him enter. Before anyone could say anything he put the hammer he was holding back inside the anorak and was gone, leaving something hanging on the wall.

A couple of members slid off their bar stools and wandered over to see what it was.

Nailed to the wall was a glass-fronted gold frame with the severed thumb mounted neatly in it – the name of the bent accountant was printed at the bottom.

Twenty-Nine

Above the river, storm clouds gathered belladonna
blue. The light over the water had dropped an octave.
Fran sat in her car waiting nervously for Mahon to call,
but when the car phone rang she started as though not
expecting it. She picked up the handset. 'Hello?'

Mahon's voice was guarded. 'You were right.'

Fran's body sagged. She didn't know what to say.
A silence folded round her.

'Fran?'

A sudden gust of rain rattled on the windscreen
bringing Fran back to her worst fears.

'He's using young kids to run the stuff round the
estates.'

This appalled Fran. 'Little bastard!'

'That's about all I could get.'

'Who's supplying him?'

'I don't know,' Mahon lied.

'Can you find out?'

'No.' Mahon's reply was flat and final.

Fran knew the risk to them both that Mahon had

taken to get what he had. She conceded and softened. 'Can we meet tonight?'

'Not tonight.'

The rain started to lash down. She looked out at the spiralling patterns on the surface of the river.

'I'm sorry, Fran.'

'If you can't you can't. It doesn't matter.' Her voice went dead. 'Nothing much matters any more.'

Mahon tried to lift her. 'What about tomorrow?'

Fran could only think about what Mahon had told her. 'This business with Davey has finished me.'

Mahon tried again. 'We'll talk about it tomorrow.'

Fran felt suddenly freed from all responsibility for her son. It was a curious mix of elation and deep despair. 'I'm going to Spain.' She waited for Mahon to respond but he didn't. Fran resented his silence. She wanted to hurt. 'With or without you.'

Mahon's phone clicked dead.

Fran, filled with regret, slowly lowered the car phone. The words stuck like a stone in her throat.

Frankie Pitillo was waiting for his washing to dry. He was smoking and reading the sports pages of a tabloid he'd found on a chair.

Davey entered and sat next to him. He looked at Frankie's bruised face and grinned. 'You look like the Christmas turkey on Boxing Day.'

Pitillo ignored the remark, dropped the cigarette and smeared it out. 'What you doin' here?'

Davey took a thick fold of notes out and held them under Frankie's nose. 'Mon-neeeey!'

Frankie looked around anxiously. There was only one other person in the laundrette, a fat black lady at the far end loading her family's washing into two

machines. Pitillo turned back to Davey. 'Put it away
you little prick!'

Davey stuffed the wedge back in a pocket. 'You got
a shake on, Frankie?'

Pitillo had always been unnerved by Davey; he was a
dead ringer for his father, same looks, same arrogance,
same twisted sense of humour. 'Look, I told you last
time was the last.'

Davey smiled. 'Don't fuck about Frankie. You say
that every time.'

Pitillo leaned into the boy and lowered his voice.
'People are startin' to ask questions about you.'

The smile decayed. 'What people?'

Pitillo glanced at the black woman again. She was
thumping one of the machines, trying to get it to go.

Davey took his shoulder and turned him. 'What
people, Frankie?'

Pitillo had no intention of telling him. 'If Pauli finds
out that I'm supplyin' you, he'll cut me a new arsehole!'

'Who's gonna tell him? You? Me?' He shrugged.
'Who else knows?'

'That's not the point,' said Pitillo.

Davey jabbed a finger in Pitillo's chest. 'That's
exactly the point. I could drop you right in it. Pauli's
not gonna do anything ter me is he? I mean, apart from
have a word.' Davey moved his head closer until his
mouth was at Pitillo's lobeless ear. 'But you . . .'
He stuck his tongue in Frankie's ear.

Pitillo snatched his head back in disgust and wiped
his ear. 'You dirty little cunt!'

Davey laughed and got up. 'I'll be in the car.' He
moved towards the door. 'Don't be long.' As he left
the laundrette the door closed with a crash.

It startled the black woman; she turned and glared
at Pitillo.

Frankie ignored her and lit another cigarette. He knew he had a problem on his hands. He was like a struggling plate spinner trying to keep his act together.

Mahon was in a phone box on the corner of a quiet street, reporting back to Lynn about his meeting with West. Call girl cards were wedged into any crack that would hold them. One was black on pink promising pain with pleasure, a crude image of long legs in black stockings, stiletto heels with spurs on them, a whip held in a gloved hand, the lash coiled like a snake round one leg. 'Mistress – dressed to thrill – silk socking and much more – credit cards accepted.'

It briefly drew Mahon's eye as he talked to Lynn. 'I thought I'd leave it a week, maybe two, then contact West.'

Lynn wasn't sure about this. 'That's playing a long game.'

Mahon knew that the closer he got to West the more cautious he had to be. 'It's taken me seven months to get this far; I don't want to start shaving the edges now.'

Lynn accepted this. 'What are you going to do?'

'Stay glued to Frankie. He's a talker.'

'How involved is he with West?' Lynn asked.

'West's his main man but he knows everyone; every supplier and dealer, the money, the front men, the crews, all the low life, the pus.'

There was something in Mahon's voice that Lynn hadn't heard before. 'Don't let it get to you, John.'

Lynn rarely used Mahon's Christian name; when he did it was usually to curb his Celtic guilt.

Mahon didn't attempt to hide his feelings. 'You can't help it when you see what I see every day. It's starting to sicken me.'

'Good.'

'What?'

'Good,' Lynn repeated.

Lynn constantly surprised Mahon. 'What's good about it?'

'It means that you haven't forgotten you're not one of them.'

'That scum!'

'It happens,' Lynn continued. 'I've seen it happen. One man I sent under cover in Belfast became a top Provo strategist.'

'This isn't Belfast,' said Mahon sourly.

'It's getting there,' Lynn said. 'At least they called it a war.'

A short silence fell between them, then Lynn returned to business. 'Your meeting with West . . . you don't seem too sure.'

Mahon locked back in. 'There was something about him . . .' he cast his mind back to the meeting, 'something not quite right.'

'What?'

'I don't know, just a feeling I had.'

'Do you think he knows something he shouldn't?'

'He wouldn't let me that close to him if he did.'

Lynn's voice became cautious. 'Keep your friends close but your enemies closer.' Through experience he probably knew better than Mahon just how unpredictable a man like Pauli West could be. 'Don't underestimate him.'

There was a moment of concern in Mahon's eyes. 'I've built the cover so slowly, so carefully, unless . . .'

Lynn could read Mahon's mind. 'None of the Drug Squad know about you. He couldn't have got anything from them.'

Mahon wasn't entirely convinced. 'Are you sure?'

Lynn's reply was brief and exact. 'You don't exist.'

Mahon dismissed the paranoia and moved on. 'One thing's certain: he's not going to let me inside until he's convinced.'

Lynn voice lightened a notch. 'Then we'd better convince him.'

'How?'

'I'll think of something.'

For a fleeting moment Mahon thought that Lynn and West would make the perfect team: they were both as cunning and dangerous as one another, they shared a coldness, a common moral corruption, neither of them gave a damn about anyone. Lynn's voice brought him out of this fanciful reverie.

'The woman.'

Mahon wasn't expecting this. He was thankful that Lynn couldn't see his reaction.

'She could be a liability with you moving closer to West. You'll probably meet her with him. That could be dangerous; he might sense something between you.'

Mahon tried to be as casual as possible. 'I'll talk to her.'

Lynn's voice took on an authoritarian tone. 'You don't need her anymore.'

Mahon's mind was racing but he said nothing.

'Get rid of her.'

Mahon remained silent.

'End it,' said Lynn as he rang off.

Mahon slowly replaced the receiver. He opened the door, stepped out and made his way down the street, his mind full of recent events. Maybe Fran was right. Maybe this was the time to get out, disappear. Those white villages in Spain were taking on a new significance for him.

Thirty

Joey Dakin, cropped hair, earring, a scar at the corner of his mouth, dressed in filthy overalls, was ripping out the exhaust system of a van up on a hydraulic lift. Music blared from a radio covered in grease balanced on the lift superstructure.

An immaculate old three point eight Jag with four young hounds in it drove into the cramped back-street garage. It was the sort of car that old sixties gangland villains used to flaunt themselves in. Three of them got out, the fourth remained in the back.

Dakin shouted above the music to them, 'You'll 'ave ter come back. We're short handed.'

They walked to the lift, one of them pressed the button to lower it.

Dakin swivelled round. 'What's your fuckin' game!'

Before he knew it he was being dragged out from under the van. He tried to defend himself. He was no slouch when it came to violence, but they beat him to the ground and kicked him half conscious.

The back door of the Jag opened and Davey stepped

out. He walked over to the lift and pressed the button
to stop it, then he knocked the radio to the ground
and stamped on it. The sudden lack of music left a
deafening silence.

Davey moved across to his crew and looked down
at Dakin. 'Remember me?'

Dakin, dazed and half-blinded with blood, tried to
say something.

Davey kicked him viciously in the face. 'I can't hear
you.' He slipped the gun from inside his jacket, bent
and rammed the muzzle under Dakin's chin, forcing
his head back. 'You stabbed me.'

Dakin wiped blood from his eyes and looked at
Davey. 'Not me.'

Davey flared. 'You!' He rammed the gun between
Dakin's arm and body, where he had been stabbed,
and fired.

Dakin roared with pain and passed out.

Davey turned and walked back to the car, his crew
followed. They got in, slammed the doors, the engine
fired and the car reversed out of the garage and away,
leaving Joey Dakin lying unconscious on the ground
in a pool of blood.

Thirty-One

Mahon was sitting at the table, folding and filling gram wraps with street heroin. The front door bell rang. The dog, lying close to his chair, got to its feet and barked. Mahon looked down at it. 'Behave.' Another ring, longer, more insistent.

Mahon got up and crossed to the window. He looked down into the street and could just see Jimmy Ryan, who had stepped back to look up at the flat. Mahon moved back to the table, scooped everything into a box and hid it behind the sofa.

The bell rang a third time as Mahon left the room.

He picked up the entry phone on the landing. 'What do you want?'

Ryan's voice crackled over the intercom. 'Got a message from Pauli West.'

'What is it?'

Ryan's voice tightened. 'Not in the street.'

Mahon pressed the door release, the lock below buzzed, the door opened and then closed. He listened for footsteps on the stairs, then called down, 'You in?'

Ryan didn't reply but then Mahon heard him coming up.

Mahon waited on the landing for Ryan to appear.

Ryan came up the last flight of stairs. One look at Mahon told him that he was a man who could handle himself. It was the way he stood; he was balanced, ready. He stepped onto the landing and faced Mahon. 'Took yer time.'

Mahon had seen Jimmy Ryan around, on the street and in the clubs, but close up he was different. It was his eyes; he'd seen those eyes before, in the queer place when he used to visit his grandma as a kid. She would dip her dentures in her tea. Mad as a bottle of bees. 'I don't have many visitors,' Mahon said, moving back to the main room.

Ryan followed him in.

The dog stood anchored on its bandy legs in the centre of the room, guarding its territory. A menacing growl came from somewhere deep in its throat.

Ryan looked at the dog, then at Mahon. 'Nasty bastards, them.'

'That's why I've got him,' Mahon said slyly. He clicked his fingers and pointed to the table. The dog went and sat quietly beside the chair, but didn't take its eyes from the intruder.

Ryan glanced round the room. It was ordered and clean but not exactly prime property. He turned to Mahon. 'How much you pay fer this?'

'Enough,' Mahon said, waiting for Ryan to deliver the message from West.

Ryan looked round again. 'They should pay you to live in this pig-pen.'

Mahon was starting not to like this man. 'What's the message?'

Ryan ignored him and moved to the framed

photographs on the walls. He looked at them. Impressed, he turned back to Mahon. 'Paras. Rough boys.'

Mahon didn't want to get into this. He lifted his jacket from the back of a chair. 'I'm on my way out.'

Ryan turned back to the photographs, pointed to one of the group. 'That you?'

Mahon pulled the jacket on.

Ryan moved on to the newspaper reports of the Falklands war. He studied them for some time then turned back to Mahon. 'You was there?'

Mahon picked up his keys from a bowl on a sideboard.

'The Falklands?'

'Yeah,' Mahon admitted reluctantly.

'Kill anyone?'

Mahon wondered how Ryan would have dealt with the freezing cold and the fear. 'Most of them were boys,' he said sympathetically.

Ryan gave Mahon a small smile, close to contempt. 'Greasy cunts. They started it!' He slipped a card from his pocket. 'Pauli's havin' a party – it's his birthday.' He held the invitation out to Mahon. 'You're invited.'

Mahon didn't take it. 'I don't go to parties.'

Ryan dropped the invitation on the floor as he turned to leave. 'Eight o'clock tomorrow night.' He moved to the door. 'Wear a suit.'

Mahon heard Ryan's footsteps down the stairs, the front door slam. He bent and picked up the invitation, looked at it. His name was spelt wrong.

The warehouse space had been cleared, a carpet laid, tables set with crisp white linen, silver cutlery, candles and flowers. Waiters moved discreetly through the press of people, serving champagne and canapés. Soft music played.

Mahon entered and hovered on the fringes, taking in the odd mix of people. Over-dressed criminals with hard-boned faces rubbed shoulders with businessmen and councillors with their dutiful wives. He recognised an MP; he had those switched-off eyes that always seemed to look slightly beyond the person he was talking to. He watched West moving graciously among his guests, chatting and joking, greeting new arrivals.

West saw Mahon and made his way over to him. 'Decided to come?'

Mahon felt ill at ease in his creased suit. 'Did I have a choice?'

West smiled and lifted a glass of champagne from the tray of a passing waiter and handed it to Mahon. 'We'll talk later.' He left Mahon and returned to stroke his guests.

Mahon let his eyes slide over the rest of the room. Seaman was with a huge man with a moustache like a palm tree. They were standing at one of the tables, looking down with a blank anxiety at the spread of gleaming cutlery, talking quietly as though trying to decide which knife to eat their peas with. Jimmy Ryan was rushing around talking to everyone like a bookie's runner. Soge, subtle as a bag of chisels, was giving a good-looking brunette the treatment. Then Mahon saw Fran. She looked pale but still beautiful. She was talking to a dodgy criminal lawyer who looked like he could pick your pocket with his tongue. Mahon knew she would be here; how to deal with it was the problem. As though she felt his eyes on her, she turned briefly and looked at him, then quickly turned back and continued the conversation.

'Beautiful woman.'

There was just a hint of threat in the voice. Mahon

turned to face J.W. He wondered if he had caught Fran's questioning glance.

'Ray Tolman's wife.'

Mahon sipped the champagne. 'Lucky man.'

J.W. ran his hand down the lapel of Mahon's jacket. 'That's a rascal of a suit.'

Mahon brushed his hand away.

'You're Mahon?'

'Yeah.'

'I know Stumpy.'

'Yeah?'

'He said you don't say much.'

Mahon placed his glass of champagne on a table and walked away from J.W. to the bar.

The barman came up to him. 'Yes, sir?'

'Do you have Irish whisky?'

As the barman moved away to pour the drink, J.W. followed Mahon to the bar. 'Pauli's got something for you.'

Mahon wasn't listening.

The barman returned with Mahon's drink. 'Ice?'

'No ice.'

'Water?'

'No water.'

J.W. didn't like being ignored. 'Did you hear me?'

Mahon went to pick up his drink.

J.W. put a hand on Mahon's arm. 'You better learn to listen.'

Mahon looked hard at J.W. 'To you?' He shook the hand from his arm, gathered his drink and brushed past him. 'I don't think so.'

The meal over, people sat at the tables smoking and talking. Fran had slipped out on to a balcony to be by herself, away from the drawn-out dullness of the conversations inside. The door slid open, Mahon stepped out and stood a few feet away looking down at the river. They ignored each other while they talked. Mahon knew an explanation was expected. 'I tried to ring you.'

To cover their conversation Fran lit a cigarette and stood with a still intensity, smoking and staring out at the city. 'I stayed over at my sister's.'

The smoke from Fran's cigarette drifted past Mahon. 'I knew you'd be here.'

Fran asked the question she had wanted to ask all night, since she first set eyes on Mahon. 'Why are *you* here?'

Mahon leaned on the balcony rail. 'He invited me.'

Fran's voice tightened. 'Why?'

'I did a job for him.'

Fran flared. 'You bloody fool!' She lowered her voice almost to a whisper. 'He's vicious and dangerous, he's sick, he'll . . .' She heard the doors slide open behind them, then West's voice.

'You'll get cold out here.'

Fran dropped the cigarette into the river and turned to him. 'I was just coming in.'

West saw that it was Mahon on the balcony with Fran. 'Have you two met?'

Mahon knew he had to offset any hint of suspicion. 'I was going to introduce myself but the lady looked like she wanted to be private.'

He moved to them and offered Fran his hand. 'John Mahon.'

They both knew this was a desperate moment, but strangely there was a feeling of excitement mixed with the fear. Fran took Mahon's hand and held it as long as she dared. 'Irish?'

Mahon smiled. 'Sort of.'

Fran let Mahon lead her into a conversation. 'Sort of?'

Mahon glanced at West. He saw that his eyes were dull with drink, not sharp with suspicion. He looked back at Fran, trying to communicate his growing confidence. 'It's a place you don't dare to have ambitions. They tried to make me stay at home but I thought the world has got to be a bigger place than Oranmore.' He paused and smiled. 'Funny lot the Irish, the crib, the cross and the empty tomb, they're usually very compliant.' He paused again and looked at West, as though his next words were a warning. 'But if you try to make them do something they don't want to, it's like trying to peel a stone.'

Fran found herself laughing and relaxing. A dark wing of hair had fallen across her face. Mahon only just stopped himself from reaching out and brushing it back.

West turned to her. He seemed in an unusually good mood. 'That's the most anyone has ever heard him say.'

Fran shivered and rubbed her bare arms. 'You're right, it's getting chilly.' She turned back to Mahon. 'I think you're missing Ireland.'

They both knew there was more to this than just the words.

Mahon had to smile. 'Perhaps.'

As West took Fran inside, Mahon turned back to the river running like a grey scar across the face of the city. He had a lingering sense of elation, as though he had found his way out of a dark wood.

All the guests were gone, just Mahon, Fran, Pauli West and his close people were left. The tables and bar were being cleared away, the carpet rolled up.

J.W. took his car keys from a pocket and turned to West. 'I'll run Fran back. Meet you later.'

As they left, West turned to Mahon. 'We need to talk.'

A thrill ran through Mahon. He knew he was in, but he managed to appear casual. 'Doesn't hurt to listen.'

Ryan was holding an unopened bottle of champagne. 'Good party, Pauli.'

West lit a cigarette. 'Not bad.'

Seaman looked puzzled. 'Lot of straight people.'

West shook his head knowingly. 'You're wrong. They're bent, but in a different way.'

Soge laughed. 'See that pratt MP? Dead Eddie bendin' his ear?'

West never missed a trick. 'I hope we got some snaps.'

West and Mahon emerged from the warehouse and made their way slowly down the river street to the cars. A distance behind them, the others left the warehouse. A dark saloon turned into the street, eased silently up the road behind them and then accelerated. Mahon snatched a glance back then grabbed West and half-ran half-hurled him on his face behind one of the parked cars. There was a dry rattle of automatic gunfire, bullets raked the wall and the car, shattering the windows.

Ryan dropped the bottle of champagne, pulled a gun and came running up the street, firing at the gunman's car as it disappeared into the darkness.

West was lying on the pavement covered in glass. Seaman arrived as he went to get up. He bent down beside him. 'Easy! Easy!'

West was shaken but unhurt. 'I'm okay.' Seaman

tried to help him up but West brushed him away. 'I'm okay!'

Mahon was lying near him, unconscious. Soge could see blood on his neck. He turned to West. 'He's not.'

West pushed Soge aside. 'Let me see.' He bent to look at Mahon, who was starting to recover consciousness.

Ryan was wound like a spring. 'Fuckin' dogs! Who was it?' He turned to the others. 'Did anyone see?'

West knelt beside Mahon and carefully brushed glass from his face. He took out a handkerchief and started to wipe blood from the neck wound. 'Doesn't look too bad.'

Ryan was losing control. 'Find the bastards! Blow their fuckin' arms and legs off!'

West glared up at him. 'Shut the fuck up, Jimmy! Shut that mouth of yours!'

Soge helped West lift Mahon to his feet. West looked at Seaman and nodded at the bullet-pocked car. 'Lose the car.'

It was Seaman's. He got into it. The starter motor whined, finally the engine fired; he dropped into gear and drove off.

Soge and West helped Mahon into the back of Ryan's car.

Ryan powered down a deserted riverside road. West and Mahon were in the back. Soge followed driving West's car. A silence had settled on them. Ryan glanced at West in the rear view mirror. 'What we gonna do, Pauli?'

West's voice was flat, unemotional. 'Nothing.'

Ryan was amazed. 'Nothin'?'

West had the handkerchief pressed to Mahon's neck. 'For a while. Let things settle.'

Ryan wound the car round a long bend heading away

from the river, putting as much distance as he could between them and the shooting before the police arrived. 'It's gotta be one of two parties. You know who they are. We come down on 'em both, full fuckin' strength!'

West was stoically calm. 'It's not the right time.'

Ryan protested. 'Right time? Right time? You gonna wait until they kill you?'

West ignored him and turned to Mahon. 'How you feeling?'

Mahon dismissed it. 'Just a nick.'

Ryan couldn't let it go. 'We gotta do something, now. Ternight, Pauli!'

West turned on him. 'Fer fucksake shut your crack, Jimmy, and drive!' He looked back at Mahon. 'How did you know?'

Mahon reached up and eased West's hand with the bloody handkerchief from his neck. 'Two tours in Belfast. I can smell a gun.' The bleeding had stopped. 'If that had been the Provos, you'd be dead.'

Thirty-Two

West's flat was sombre, almost clubbish; none of the cash and flash usually associated with successful criminals. He stood at an antique drinks cabinet pouring two whiskies, his back to Mahon who was sitting in an armchair, a dressing on his neck. 'Jimmy's got to go.' He brought the drinks across. 'He's out of control.' He handed Mahon his whisky. 'He's no use to me like that.'

Mahon sipped his whisky; it was a fine malt. 'We had one like him in Belfast; went crazy one night. Shot up a car, killed three kids.'

West settled in a chair and raised his glass to Mahon. 'Thanks.'

Mahon's head was aching like hell; it was as though his eyes were bandaged with barbed wire. He laid his drink aside and massaged his temples.

'Feeling rough?'

Mahon felt the dressing on his neck. 'A bit sore.'

West downed his whisky and got up to freshen his glass. 'I need a middle-man, someone intelligent who can read people. You've got a way with you, with words. You're easy, you can talk, explain things.' He poured the whisky then turned back to Mahon. 'You don't talk much but when you do people listen. I've noticed.' He paused. 'Take Fran tonight.'

Mahon felt a shard of anxiety at the mention of Fran, but he had learned to use anxiety. 'Your friend on the balcony?'

West sat back in his chair. 'You made her laugh. She hasn't laughed for a long while.'

Mahon realised he got a lift talking about Fran in the abstract. 'I liked her.'

West moved on. 'I want to set you up: decent place to live, decent car, expenses.' He pointed at Mahon's crumpled ten-year-old suit and smiled. 'If you're gonna work for me the wardrobe might need a little attention.'

Mahon knew that he couldn't drop into this offer too easily. 'I've got people to look after.'

West sipped his whisky. 'I'll see they're alright.'

Mahon shook his head. 'No.'

'Give them to Frankie,' West suggested.

Mahon's concern for his clients was genuine. 'Frankie's an addict. He's careless. He's gonna get pulled. He'll offer them up.'

West tightened. 'Not Frankie.'

'Have you ever seen a heavy user held in a cell for two days?'

West was getting frustrated. 'You're a stubborn bastard.'

Mahon accepted this. 'And then some.'

West looked at Mahon and conceded. 'Okay. Keep your people, but our business comes first.'

Mahon wanted to move into the details. 'What is "our business"?'

West, ever cautious, finished his drink. 'You'll
soon learn.'

Mahon pushed it. 'How do you know you can trust
me?' For one stalled second Mahon thought he had
dropped it as he saw West's reaction.

West sat rooted in silence, then pointed to Mahon's
neck wound. 'You took one for me – you didn't have
to. You helped Frankie out with that scum – you didn't
have to. You took the half, not the bag, for the Essex run.
I liked that. You're loyal to your people; you could've
dumped them and you didn't. Because you're giving
me a hard time convincing you. Because you look me
in the eye. But one wrong move and they'll find you
face down in a ditch.'

Mahon sat exhausted and melancholy in the back of
a taxi, watching the irreversible decay of the inner
city pan past as the cab clattered its way along the
deserted streets. He tried to trace his life back to
when he got caught up in this insanity, and wondered
when he would return to a more manageable life. He
had often wondered why people didn't just walk away
from lives that were becoming untenable, but now he
was starting to realise that he was trapped by his own
obsession with Pauli West and all those other soulless
vermin who left fragments of shattered lives behind
them. He wanted to cut them out like a cancer. This
obsession had become both the knife and the wound.
The scent of the city was on him and he knew that he
could not wash it away with hate.

Mahon made his way wearily up the stairs to his flat.
As he opened the door the air around him tensed, just as
it had on those freezing night patrols in the Falklands.
In the pale light that bled into the flat from a street lamp,

he saw someone sitting in a chair, the dog asleep on the floor beside him. He switched the light on.

It was Lynn.

Mahon looked first at the dog then at Lynn.

'I have a way with dogs.'

The dog stirred in its sleep and yawned, showing the white blades of its teeth.

Mahon slipped his coat off. 'You must have. Normally he'd have your bastard arm off.'

Beside the dog stood a bottle of Bushmills that Mahon had only recently opened.

Lynn drained his glass and took in Mahon's condition. 'I told them to aim as low as possible without killing you both.'

Mahon absently raised a hand to the bloody dressing on his neck. 'I took a ricochet.'

Lynn reached down for the bottle, poured a drink and held it out to Mahon. 'That must have looked convincing?'

Mahon took the glass and sipped the whisky. He accepted the fact that Lynn was an ice-hearted bastard. 'The whole thing was.'

Lynn dropped a hand and rubbed the sleeping dog behind the ear. 'It worked then? Worked out well?'

The exhaustion and depression that Mahon had felt transformed into a surge of excited enthusiasm at the brilliance of the scam that Lynn had devised. 'You should've seen them – totally fucked! West was shaking. Face the colour of a cheap envelope.'

'What was his reaction?' Lynn asked.

'It wasn't so much his reaction as Jimmy Ryan: he wanted to kill everyone.'

Lynn got up from the chair and went into the small kitchen. He soon returned with another glass. 'We used a counter-gang operation like this in Belfast in seventy-one.' He picked up the bottle and poured himself a drink. 'Had the Provos killing their own people.'

Mahon had thought it through. 'West won't make a move until he knows exactly who and what was involved, but Ryan, he's got a serious thinking disorder. He's the trigger on this.'

Lynn sat back in the chair. 'Can you get to him?'

'I don't want to go near him. Pauli's got him down as a problem. Can't we feed him a name from the street? From someone he trusts?'

Lynn considered it.

'We could use Frankie Pitillo. He's got friends in the Drug Squad. Use one of them to float a name. We know Pauli West's main rivals – give him one of them.'

Lynn deferred to Mahon. 'Which one?'

Mahon didn't have to think too hard. 'Venner.'

'Why Venner?'

'He hates Pauli's guts.'

Lynn wanted this right. 'Enough to attempt a shooting?'

Mahon swallowed what remained of the whisky. 'Oh yes.'

Lynn raised his glass to Mahon. 'Let's start a war!'

Thirty-Three

Frankie Pitillo walked down a quiet backstreet. A car slowed beside him and the driver talked to Frankie as he kept on the move. Pitillo stopped, the car stopped and he got in.

He settled on the seat beside Danny Fitt. 'What is this, Danny?'

Fitt accelerated away. 'You're nicked, my old beauty.'

Frankie was about to light a cigarette. 'What!'

Fitt took the cigarette from Pitillo's lips and stuck it in his mouth. 'Sorry, Frankie. That's the way it is.'

Pitillo couldn't believe it. 'What for?'

Fitt took a lighter from his pocket and lit the cigarette. 'You've been playing Alsatians with this married sort. We found her old man dead on the floor of their bedroom.'

Pitillo was speechless with astonishment.

Fitt grinned. 'She says you hit him with a golf club.'

Frankie exploded with indignation. 'What's her name?'

'Alice Cook.'

'Slag Alice! I haven't seen her for months,' Pitillo protested. 'She's tryin' ter stick it on me.'

Fitt blared his horn at the car in front to move over. He accelerated past it and turned back to Pitillo. 'She's a tough turn. She's put you right in it.' He shook his head mournfully. 'This is a bad do, Frankie.'

Pitillo saw that Fitt was desperately trying not to laugh. 'Are you winding me up?'

Fitt started to laugh.

Frankie was not amused.

By now Fitt was choking with laughter.

'You evil bastard!' Frankie tempered his anger. The laughter was infectious and he started to see the funny side of it, more out of relief than anything else. 'You had me goin' there, Danny.'

Fitt scrubbed tears from his eyes. 'I did, didn't I? Your fuckin' face!'

Pitillo started to relax. He took out his cigarettes and lit one. 'So . . . you got somethin' for me?'

Fitt became serious. 'Let's go somewhere quiet.'

Danny Fitt was well named; he'd fit up anyone. He had rodent eyes and a mouth that looked like he'd been giving the kiss of life to a ferret. He was one of the old style filth: a bone breaker, a liberty taker, bent to buggery. There wasn't a week went by that he didn't take a sweetener from someone. Even his close friends couldn't work out how he had made it into the Drug Squad. It was like putting a fox in a chicken run.

Fitt drove into a football stadium car park, stopped, switched the ignition off and turned to Pitillo. 'That bit of naughty the other night.'

Frankie was wary. 'What was that then?'

'I heard it was a close thing.'

Frankie lit another cigarette. 'I don't know what you're talkin' about.'

'Pauli West was nearly no more.'

Frankie continued with the sparring. 'Talk me out of my doubts about you, Danny.'

Fitt shook his head solemnly. 'Bad business.' Fitt knew he was on solid ground for at least a grand. 'I've got a name.'

Pitillo wasn't expecting this. 'Who?'

Fitt grinned: he knew he had him. 'I thought you didn't know nothin' about it?'

Pitillo dropped the pretence. 'Fer fucksake Danny! This name?'

Fitt lifted the lit cigarette from Frankie's fingers, took a drag and passed it back. 'Venner.'

A black kid with etched hair whirred up and down the canyons of cartons on a rusting yellow forklift, stacking orders in a wine warehouse that West owned.

Soge was checking stock sheets on a clipboard.

Pitillo entered.

Soge saw him and came over. 'What are you doin' here?'

Frankie turned to check that the forklift was not too close. 'Looking fer Pauli. Is he around?'

Soge didn't much like working. He tossed the clipboard on top of a case of wine. 'No.'

Frankie was disappointed. He was expecting to find West here. 'Where is he? It's important.'

Soge knew it must be; he'd never known Frankie to come to the warehouse before. 'What's up?'

Pitillo didn't have much time for Soge; he was too full of himself. 'D'yer know where I can reach him?'

Soge didn't care much for Frankie either. 'He said he'd be back later. I don't know where he's gone.'

Pitillo turned to leave.

Soge put a hand on his arm. 'If he rings in what shall I tell him?'

'I'll ring him ternight.' Pitillo started for the door then stopped and turned back. 'Is Jimmy around?'

When the body of Nicky Mobbs was found, rats had eaten half his face. He was identified by his fingerprints. The murdered corpse found at the landfill site made a strong story for the inside pages of the tabloids. The usual *insider* information about gangland killings was pumped out by a tacky journalist who'd dropped a detective sergeant at the local factory a drink and got some details. A few faces were being pulled in and questioned, but generally the feeling among the police was that Nicky Mobbs was a piece of shit and would be mourned by no one – fucking good riddance.

Alan Mercer was feeling edgy. Everything had been going so well up to now; his contacts on the Continent were ready to blitz the UK with massive shipments of drugs, he would distribute, make a fortune, get out, go abroad with his family. At least that was the plan. The execution of Nicky Mobbs closely followed by the shooting on the river road were disturbing. The violence was escalating. When a war between rival crews broke out this is how it started. He had seen it all before. Mercer had spent months bringing the major players together. It hadn't been easy; like predatory animals they were fiercely territorial. If the whole deal wasn't to blow up in his face, Alan Mercer had to know exactly what was going on. The only one who could tell him this was Pauli West.

'What's this I hear about a shooting?'

'It's nothing.'

'That's not what I heard.'

'You know what it's like; a gun is only a phone call away. Some little snot out to make a name for himself.'

'Nothing to do with Nicky Mobbs?'

The question surprised West. He had never considered this. 'Nicky?'

'You tell me he was working both corners, you and Venner, so you kill him. The next thing I hear about is this shooting. Automatic weapons – that's no little snot out to make a name for himself, that is serious violence!'

'It wasn't Venner.'

'How do you know?'

'Because he knows it could fuck up this deal.'

'It could.'

'And secondly he's not going to bang heads with me over a piece of dirt like Nicky Mobbs.'

'If it wasn't Venner, who was it?'

'I don't know – yet.'

'I hear you've been putting the hand on people.'

'Who told you that?'

'Squeezing people.'

'Who said that?'

'Firat.'

'You don't listen to him do you?'

'He's part of the deal.'

'He's a lying piece of shit!'

'Listen, Pauli. The last thing we need right now is a war!'

'I know that! But I tell you something: when this is all over, I'm gonna gut that fucking Turk!

Frankie had found Jimmy Ryan. They sat at a table in a wine bar that West supplied, where drinks were always on the house. Pitillo was one of the few faces that Ryan

trusted. He knew he had good sources: fit-up Danny Fitt
was the best – he was expensive but he'd never steered
Frankie wrong.

When Pitillo gave Ryan the name he became agitated. 'I knew it! I told Pauli!'

A young couple carried their drinks to a table nearby.
Ryan turned to them. 'That's taken.' The guy glanced
at Jimmy but didn't question it.

They moved on to the next table. Ryan gave them
a look, 'So's that.' This time the guy was just about
to say something when the girl stopped him. As they
carried their drinks to the other end of the bar Ryan
turned back to Pitillo. 'I fuckin' told him, Frankie!'

Pitillo lit a cigarette. 'What did Pauli say?'

'Wants ter wait.' Ryan looked disgusted. 'You don't
wait with people like that, you have their fuckin'
eyes!'

Pitillo tried to calm him. 'I'll go and see him.'

Ryan knew what he had to do. 'You keep out of it.
This is between me and Pauli.'

Pauli West didn't encourage callers. He wasn't pleased
when Ryan rang his bell.

Jimmy Ryan had grown up with Pauli West and
Ray Tolman. Even when they were kids local people
had christened them 'The Wild Bunch'. But now, with
Tolman in prison and West moving into a different
class of criminality, their working relationship was
becoming strained.

'I'm busy, Jimmy.'

'Not too busy for this.'

'What?'

'Danny Fitt's been talkin' to Frankie.'

'What about?'

'The shootin''

'What about it?'

'Venner – it was Venner.'

West shook his head. 'No.'

This wasn't the reaction Jimmy was expecting. 'I'm tellin' you Pauli, it was Venner.'

West fixed Ryan with a look. 'I'm telling you it wasn't.'

'Danny wouldn't offer this up if he wasn't . . .'

West cut him off. 'He got it wrong.'

Ryan reacted. 'He's never been wrong before.'

'He is this time.'

'You know who it was?'

'No.'

'Then how do you know he's wrong?'

'I don't want any move made on Venner or any of his people.'

Ryan was mystified. 'What is all this Pauli?'

'You stay away from Venner and his crew. You hear me?'

'It don't make sense.'

'Sense?'

'Well, does it?

'That's good coming from you, Jimmy.'

Ryan was confused. 'What?'

'Sense,' West repeated.

'What?'

'Making sense.'

'What?'

West crossed to the window and looked out. 'Does most of what you do make sense? Most of what you do is idiotic. Most of the time you're a liability.'

Ryan was lost. 'What?'

West turned angrily from the window. 'Don't keep saying "What?" like a fuckin' moron – at least attempt to form sentences.'

Ryan hadn't expected it to work out this way. 'You give people like Venner an inch, it's over. If they think you've gone soft they'll cut your fuckin' heart out!'

West crossed to the drinks cabinet, calmly opened it, lifted out a decanter and poured himself a drink. 'Go away, Jimmy.'

'It's on the street already.'

'Just go away.'

'If you don't come up with somethin,' every piece of dirt with a gun and a grudge is gonna come lookin' for you.'

West turned back to him. 'I couldn't start to explain, Jimmy. You're not intelligent enough to grasp it.' He sipped his whisky as he returned to face Ryan. 'Let me do the thinking. You're not capable. You're a hammer, Jimmy, and that's all you are. You'll never be anything else. You were born without a brain.'

West had never talked to Ryan like this before. It went deep.

Ryan reacted. 'At least I'm a man.' He turned and made his way to the door. It had been raining; there were wet footprints on the carpet from when he had come in.

West pointed to them. 'Look at my carpet.'

Ryan couldn't believe it. He turned back.

West pointed again. 'Look at it.'

Ryan looked. 'Oh dear! Oh fuckin' dear! I forgot to wipe my feet.' He looked up at West. 'I am sorry.' He smiled – then unzipped and pissed on the carpet.

Thirty-Four

Tony Venner and his cousin Dave Newis were driving back from a charity black-tie boxing dinner. They were well flavoured, singing along to an old Desmond Dekker tape. This was their era. They started young and rose fast. At sixteen they were already terrorising their neighbourhood, collecting insurance from local shops and pubs, putting the black on illegal immigrants, and several other nasty but profitable little tucks. Through the years their criminal scope had widened. Now they were firmly established as two of the top men in drug importation and distribution in the city. The only man that Venner feared was West. There was something about Pauli that made your flesh crawl, and he was a thinker; he always seemed to be on the next page. Venner had heard about the shooting and he wondered who had the sand to try it. Probably those crazy Turks from north London. They had a shaming difficulty with sharing their territory; if you stepped over their line they wanted to know why. He knew that the way things had been going lately with West squeezing the opposition, someone had to take a pop at him. He'd thought about it himself but he knew what the consequences would be if it failed: Pauli West would perform open heart surgery on you and go in through your feet. He pitied the poor sod who'd pulled that trigger.

A car pulled alongside, the passenger window lowered and Jimmy Ryan emptied a gun at them. Newis took it in the face. Venner raised a hand as if trying to fend off the bullet that went through it.

Ryan checked the rear view mirror as he accelerated away. He saw the heavy saloon go out of control, smash into a parked van, jump the kerb, power across the pavement and plough into a shop front. Pilled up to the eyeballs, he roared his satisfaction like a madman, brandishing the empty gun out of the window.

Shattered glass was still falling from what was left of the shop front as the passenger door of the wrecked saloon opened and Venner staggered out, covered in blood and clutching his crippled hand. Newis sat dead in the driver's seat, half his face missing, a sheet of blood down the front of his dress shirt.

The tape continued to play . . . *you can get it if you really want it.*

Thirty-Five

It was nearly dawn when Davey got home. He entered and switched on the hall light.

Fran appeared at the top of the stairs in a dressing gown and stood there looking down at her son, in the hope of dispelling some of the emptiness inside her. 'When you were born, when the nurse put you in my arms, I thought you were the most beautiful thing I had ever seen.'

Davey stood stranded in the hallway.

'I loved you so much it hurt, it physically hurt.'

He could see that she was drunk. He had never seen his mother drunk before.

'I promised myself that it was going to be different with you. I was going to make it different.'

Davey moved to the bottom of the stairs and looked up at her. 'You're drunk.'

Fran ignored him. 'You were going to be the one good thing in my life. All the rest was . . . was nothing, empty, no life at all.' She took her hands from behind her back. They were full of the money she had found in the box.

Davey started angrily up the stairs. 'Where did you get that?'

Before he could get to her Fran started to throw the money down into the hallway. Davey tried to grab what was left.

'Is this all you want out of life? Like him? Money?' The notes spiralled down and settled on the hall floor. She thrust her face close to his. Her breath was hot and sour. 'Has he corrupted you that much? Your father? That pig!'

'Shut your mouth!'

'God I wish he was dead!'

'Shut your fucking mouth!'

'I hope he dies in prison.'

Davey hit her.

Fran lost her balance, went tumbling down and lay curled like a question mark at the bottom of the stairs.

Before he left the house, Davey stopped and looked briefly back, as though the woman lying unconscious on the floor was someone he knew, but barely.

Fran spent most of the day in bed, just lying there thinking. She knew she couldn't continue in this limbo. She had to make a decision what to do. If Mahon had said he would go to Spain they could have been there by now, but Fran sensed there was something holding him in this sewer of a city, something dark and elusive that he was careful to conceal.

It was late afternoon when Fran got up and called Mahon. 'I've got to see you . . . tonight . . .' Fran continued, unaware that Davey had come into the house the back way and was hidden, listening to every word. All that she could think of was seeing Mahon. 'You *will* be there?'

*   *   *

As Fran left the house a kid on a mountain bike passed her, bouncing up on the pavement then back down onto the road. She turned the corner, got to her car, unlocked it and got in. The boy on the bike rode past in the opposite direction as Fran went to take the wig from the glove box. She put it back, took the keys to the flat and dropped them in her bag.

As Fran drove off a car eased out from a side road and followed. The boy watched the two cars as they both turned at the end of the road. He took out a mobile and pressed a pre-set number. 'Davey, it's Dean. She's on her.'

Fran had noticed a car following behind for some time. She'd checked the driver in her rear view mirror when they stopped at lights: seventeen, blonde, eyes you could swim in. Fran supposed the girl was seen as beautiful, seen that is through the vacant lens of a camera. She had the intense self-preoccupation of a model as she painted her lips a soft sin red, using the mirror on the back of the sun visor to check her hasty maquillage. Fran was not unduly worried but she found herself feeling relieved when the car seemed no longer to be there.

As Fran took the keys from her bag and opened the door to the flat, she didn't notice the same car edge into the end of the street.

The girl drove slowly past the antique shop. She saw the light in the flat above come on. She picked up her mobile from the passenger seat. 'Davey?'

Fran sat smoking nervously, waiting for Mahon. She heard the front door open and close quietly, then footsteps on the creaking stairs.

Mahon entered looking concerned. 'What's happened?'

'You ask me that?' Fran angrily stabbed her cigarette
out. 'You're shot, nearly killed. That bastard hasn't got
a scratch on him and you ask me that? You tell me
you're working for Pauli West. What do you know
about him? Nothing! Only what you've heard and you
haven't heard the half of it! You're going to end up in
prison. Worse still, crippled or dead!'

Sam had parked at the end of the road. Davey's
BMW pulled up behind her. Sam left her car and got
into his.

'A big guy went in.'

'What d'he look like?'

Sam shrugged. 'I didn't really . . .'

Davey was edgy. 'You saw him!'

'It was dark!' Sam protested.

Davey calmed and lit two cigarettes; passed one to
her. 'How long ago?'

'Just after she went in.' Sam checked her watch.
'Twenty minutes.'

Davey settled back in his seat. 'So – we wait.'

'She'll see your car won't she?' Sam asked. 'Your
mother?'

Davey blew smoke at her. 'She don't know I've got
it.'

'I know these people. I grew up with these people. I'm
married to one of the worst of them. I know how they
think, how they work, just how dangerous they can be.'
Fran lit another cigarette. 'Pauli sucks people in, uses
them. Ray was always a criminal, I knew that when I
married him, but he wasn't into drugs. Ray's doing the
fifteen years that Pauli should be doing. I wish to God
he had been shot. If you hadn't been there he might
have been killed – the wicked bastard!'

Mahon poured two glasses of whisky from a bottle he kept at the flat. 'You don't understand.'

'Understand what?'

'You don't know what's involved.'

Fran sipped the whisky. 'What do you mean, involved? What do you mean? What are you saying?'

Mahon was on the edge of telling Fran about himself, Lynn, the whole bloody business, but he drew back. 'Nothing'. He drank his whisky. 'I don't know what I'm saying.' He went to move away. 'Forget it.'

She stopped him. 'Tell me.'

Lies flew easily to Mahon's tongue. 'There's nothing to tell.'

They'd been waiting an hour. Sam was painting her nails the same seductive red as her lips. 'What you gonna do, Davey?'

He wasn't expecting the question. 'What?'

'When you know who he is.'

Davey's expression hardly changed. 'Kill him.'

Sam giggled nervously. 'No . . . serious?'

Davey gave Sam a look as if it made perfect sense.

Fran looked round the room as though only now realising how shabby it was. 'I hate this city. I've got to get out before it kills that part of me that's still worth something.' She had never reached such airless depths before. 'Davey was the one thing I thought I could believe in. He'll be in prison by the time he's twenty, just like his father. I'm not going to wait around for that. I don't think I could face that. I'm going away. If you won't come with me I'll go alone.'

A wing of hair had fallen across her face. Fran softened. 'Come with me, John.'

Mahon reached out and brushed it back. 'I can't.'

She took his hand. 'Why? I've got money, enough for both of us.'

'It's not money.'

'Is it Pauli? Has he got something on you?'

Mahon shook his head. 'No.'

'That's the way that swine works.'

'It's not that.'

'Why can't you tell me?'

Mahon slipped his hand from Fran's. 'I've got to go.'

Fran's voice curled away. 'If you walk out of that door you'll never see me again.'

Sam spotted Mahon as he left the flat and walked down the street towards them. She nudged Davey. 'Here he comes.'

Mahon was lost in thought as he closed on the car.

Davey opened his door and got out. 'S'cuse me . . .'

Mahon almost collided with him.

Davey gave him a calculating, affable smile. 'Do you know if there's a restaurant round here called . . .'

Mahon cut him off and eased past. 'I'm not from around here, sorry.'

Davey got a good look at Mahon under the street light, and he'd noted the accent. He stood watching him move on down the street with a lazy loping gait, then turn a corner.

Sam saw Fran leave. She called anxiously to Davey, 'Get in!'

Davey looked at Sam. She pointed up the road and he saw his mother starting towards him. He dropped back into the car and closed the door.

Sam coiled herself around him, kissing him, hiding his face.

Fran passed close without a glance then crossed the road to her car.

Davey stared past Sam at his mother. She sat in the car, her face pale and pinched, going over in her mind what had happened between her and Mahon. She couldn't quite believe it was finished, that she might never see him again. She gathered herself, started the car, switched the lights on and drove away.

Davey pushed Sam away. 'Do you know what she said to me?' His voice filled with scorn. 'My darling mother?' He took out his cigarettes. 'That she wished my old man was dead. That she hopes he dies in prison.' He lit two and passed one to Sam. 'Lovely eh?' An unmanageable rage was spawning in Davey. 'She prefers some Irish pigfucker to my father!'

Thirty-Six

Women said J.W. looked like Mr Tibbs. They couldn't remember the name of the actor but he was a good-looking man, just like J.W. That was before three of Tony Venner's crew went to work on him. They dragged him into a van, drove to a garage Venner owned and beat him near senseless.

Tony Venner, his injured hand wired to a metal splint resting in a sling, stood looking down at J.W. lying in a pool of oil on the garage floor. He could see the white of the skull beneath the flesh where his head had been sliced open with an iron bar. 'That nonce Jimmy Ryan tried to kill me! He shot Dave Newis in the face!' J.W. tried to say something but his mouth was too swollen. 'This wasn't Pauli's doing. He's a lying, scheming pig but I know he didn't want this. He doesn't want a war; there's too much at stake.' The men lifted J.W. to his feet. 'I want that brainsick bastard Ryan or it's goin' off between me and Pauli, got it?'

J.W. managed a nod.

Venner eased his injured hand in the sling. 'You tell Pauli that.'

A car approached six isolated beach houses and stopped a distance away; the lights were switched off. In the darkness beyond sand dunes covered in sea grass, the incoming tide crashed in then hissed back down the beach. West got out and made his way to the first of the houses. He saw Ryan's car parked behind it. He knew Jimmy wouldn't be hard to find; he was a creature of habit, a dog who returns to its vomit. Whenever he was in trouble he came down here to hide. West made his way to the back door. It wasn't locked.

He entered.

Moonlight filtered through the salt-etched windows. West made his way through a geometry of shadows to a flight of wooden stairs and silently started to climb them.

In one of the rooms, Jimmy Ryan was lying fully-dressed on the bed in a drunken stupor, a blanket pulled carelessly over him. The gun used in the shooting lay close to hand.

West entered and stood like a bird of prey in his black coat looking down at him. He picked up Ryan's gun and checked it was loaded. As he slipped the pillow from beneath Ryan's head he stirred but didn't wake. West held the pillow over his face, dug the muzzle of the gun into it to muffle the blast, and shot Ryan twice in the head.

He removed the singed pillow and stripped the blanket away, then with the cold focus of a psychopath he carefully arranged the body in a crucifixion: feet together, arms outstretched, a dark halo of blood circling what was left of the head.

West stepped back to admire the effect then slipped a

Polaroid camera from his pocket, opened it and looked
through the viewfinder to compose an image of this
criminal Christ.

The flash scorched the room.

The dog was curled up on the bed with Mahon. The
telephone woke them both. The dog wheezed a growl
then went back to sleep as Mahon fumbled for the
receiver in the darkness. 'Yeah?' He was still in that
limbo between sleeping and waking. 'What now?'
He switched a lamp on and rubbed his face awake.
'Where?'

Mahon drove into the deserted supermarket car park
and switched off the lights and engine. Townes Van
Zandt played softly – *maybe she just has to sing for
the sake of the song . . .*

West's car pulled in and parked alongside.

They both got out.

West heard the music. 'Shut that off!'

Mahon reached into his car and turned the tape
off.

West took a sealed envelope from his pocket with
Venner's name and address printed on the front. 'I
want you to deliver this.'

Mahon took the envelope.

'He's expecting you.'

Mahon glanced at the name, then at Pauli West.
'Why me?'

'Introduce yourself.'

Mahon looked at the name again. 'I hear he's a
Christian.'

West slipped Ryan's gun from his pocket. 'You can
handle him.'

He held the gun out and smiled. 'Can't you?'

Mahon knew West was testing him, looking for fear like looking for scratches on glass.

Mahon took the automatic and checked it. The clip was two rounds short.

West pointed at the sealed envelope. 'When he's seen it, burn it.'

As he drove through the sleeping city, Mahon slipped the envelope from his pocket and looked at it front and back. He had to know what was in it. He pulled over and stopped, took out a penknife and patiently teased the flap of the envelope open. The polaroid crucifixion was certainly not what Mahon was expecting. Now he knew where the missing two rounds were – in Jimmy Ryan's head.

At the house Venner gave Mahon a slow up-and-down look. 'You must be Pauli's new boy.'

Mahon didn't reply. He took the envelope from a pocket and passed it to him.

Venner tore open the envelope, took out the Polaroid and looked at it for some moments.

Mahon waited for a reaction but there wasn't one. Maybe the frozen photographic image of violent death was not real enough for Venner; too stilted and inert. Maybe it was *too* real, and Venner's face was showing a blank acceptance that this is the way it is, the way it has to be – one shattered head for another.

Venner slipped the polaroid back in the envelope and went to put it in his pocket.

'He told me to burn it.'

Venner half turned to go back in.

Mahon eased forward. 'He said to burn it.'

Venner wanted him gone. 'Tell Pauli I'll see him tomorrow.'

Mahon slipped the gun from his belt and levelled it at Venner. 'He said burn it as soon as you'd seen it.'

There was a stillness in the quiet Irishman that Venner found unsettling. He slowly passed the envelope back.

Mahon stuck the gun back in his belt, took out a lighter and set fire to the corner of the envelope. He dropped the last flaming piece on the ground, rubbed the ash into powder with a foot, then turned and walked away with a long easy stride.

The next morning Mahon met with Lynn at the hotel. The plan Lynn had devised to start an internecine war between West and Venner had taken an unexpected turn. It was puzzling.

Lynn was trying to work it out. 'Ryan attempts to shoot Venner, kills Newis. Then West kills Ryan.'

Mahon checked Lynn. 'We don't know that.'

'You've got the gun.'

'I've got *a* gun.'

Lynn dismissed Mahon's caution. 'The gun, the polaroid. West killed Ryan – but why? A life for a life? Ryan for Newis? The polaroid to prove he was dead? But why? They hate each other's guts. It's poison between them. Why would West take all that trouble to kill Ryan, a man he grew up with, then photograph him, and get you out of your bed to deliver the picture of the dead man to Tony Venner?'

'Trying to keep Venner sweet?' Mahon suggested.

Lynn was knotted with frustration. 'But why? Why? Why?'

Mahon had lain awake all night thinking about it. 'What if there was something going down, something special, something that both West and Venner are involved in?'

Lynn picked up on Mahon's theory. 'Something all the major players are involved in?'

'And it's just about to go off.' Mahon added.

Lynn was into it. 'No one wants trouble. They're all on their best behaviour. It's a truce. Common cause – money! They can resume killing each other later.'

It was starting to make sense to Mahon. 'Then we come along just at the wrong time and blow holes in their truce – literally.'

Lynn moved into the details. 'Ryan's a madhead.'

Mahon batted it back. 'He doesn't know about the deal.'

'West tries to reel him in.'

'He gets pilled up, goes after Venner.'

'Kills his cousin.'

'Venner tells West the game's over unless he gets Jimmy Ryan.'

Lynn liked what he was hearing. 'West wouldn't leave that to anyone else.'

Mahon agreed. 'Too much explaining to do.'

Lynn was buzzing. 'We've got West for murder. Maybe we can turn him, use him. Find out what's going on.'

For once Lynn wasn't thinking straight. Mahon pointed this out. 'You try that with West and I'm out in the open. I'm the only one who knows Jimmy Ryan is dead apart from Venner and West.'

'He doesn't know you saw the polaroid.'

'It wouldn't take him too long to work it out.'

'Why did he get you to deliver it? Why didn't he go himself?'

Mahon had thought about this. 'I don't know.'

'Why not one of the others?'

'He didn't want them involved.'

Lynn checked his watch as though he was late for

another appointment. 'We need that body. Try to find out where the killing was.'

Lynn made the impossible sound casual.

'That won't be easy.'

Lynn's voice tightened. 'Did I suggest it would be?'

Thirty-Seven

Just pre-dawn, in the pewter light a small fishing boat rose and fell on a heavy swell beside a Dutch coaster. Boxes were being off loaded. A second fishing boat was anchored in a deserted bay; an inflatable was transferring the boxes to shore where a Land Rover up to its axles in water was waiting. Armed men stood guard on the dunes. This was the Irish connection: shipments of drugs were landed on remote parts of the west coast then brought across to Liverpool, Manchester and London.

Joe Crinion, an old Provo man, watched over the transfer of the shipment. That night, before the arrival of the Dutch coaster, someone he trusted had told him something that he knew he had to speak to Alan Mercer about.

Mercer was surprised by the call. 'Joe? Long time.'

'Is your phone safe?'

'Yes.'

'Sure?'

'Yes.'

'Something I think you should know, Alan.'

'What?'

'I've heard a whisper. Someone reliable. There's a security unit working with the Drug Squad and Customs over there.'

Mercer knew about the gradual infiltration of security into police work. 'There's a lot of these new groupings.'

'This one's headed by a madman called Lynn.'

Mercer hadn't heard the name. 'Lynn?'

'James Lynn. Was a major in 39 Infantry brigade in Belfast in the early seventies.'

'You sound like you know this man.'

'Everyone who was anyone then knows about Jack Lynn. He was a bastard. The bogeyman of the Provos; illegal interrogation techniques, illegal killings and counter gang operations.' He paused. 'Know what they are?'

'No.'

'You plant false information, black propaganda, con the enemy, get them killing each other.'

The conversation had started to take on a significance for Mercer.

Joe Crinion continued. 'Lynn has a talent bordering on genius for this.'

That same morning West and Venner met with Mercer at his country house. Mercer was well aware that the bond of money can be stronger and longer lasting than anything more honourable. But things weren't right. They all knew it but they weren't sure why. The recent deaths of Dave Newis and Jimmy Ryan were part of something none of them really understood. The phone call from Dublin had made a great deal of sense to Mercer. He looked between them. 'Have you thought why all this should be happening now? Just as we're getting up and running, getting it organised.'

West was confused. 'What do you mean?'

Mercer took out his snuff box. 'Joe Crinion rang me from Dublin. He's an old Provo man, he knows all about dirty tricks. He's heard a rumour that a security unit are working with the police, led by a retired army officer called Lynn, Jack Lynn.' He looked between the two of them again for any sign that the name meant something. 'He was a major in Belfast in the early seventies. He used counter gang operations.'

'What are they?' Venner asked.

'It's basically a con, a scam. You feed people false information. You put the poison in. They start killing each other,' Mercer took a pinch of snuff, 'like rats in a sack.' He turned to West. 'That shooting after your party – that could have been staged by Lynn's people.'

West could hardly believe this. 'You mean . . . ?'

The more he thought about it the more sense it made to Mercer. 'You thought what you were meant to think – it had to be one of two or maybe three crews.'

It was starting to fall into place for Pauli West. 'Then someone whose trusted drops a name?'

Venner was starting to lock in. 'Fit-up Danny Fitt.'

'Fed to them by a contact of Lynn's.'

'In the Drug Squad.' West added.

Mercer dropped the snuff box back in his waistcoat pocket. 'That's what started this whole bloody mess off. We've got two bodies; it could've been more.'

West shifted uneasily. 'If you're right it means someone's into us. This bastard Lynn must have some-one close to us.'

Mercer looked hard at him. 'Close to you, Pauli.'
West reacted. 'Why me?'

'Because it was you who was set up. It has to be someone close to you.' Mercer turned back to the window. 'You better find out who it is before he does real damage.'

West sat at a table with a cup of coffee in the empty club bar, thinking through what Mercer had said. He knew that none of his immediate people were capable of something like this: they weren't bright enough, and anyway he'd known them since God was a boy. In his mind he slowly sifted through the events of that night of the party. His suspicion started to settled on Mahon; all this had started since he met the quiet Irishman. He picked up his coffee. It was cold.

Davey entered the bar and made his way over to Pauli.

West hadn't seen the boy for months. Over the years he had watched him grow ever more like his father. It was uncanny. 'Could be your father walking in.'

Davey pulled out a chair and sat opposite.

'How's your mother?'

'Leavin'.'

This disturbed West. 'What do you mean?'

Davey took out his cigarettes. 'Says she's goin' on holiday.'

'When?'

'This afternoon.'

'Where?'

Davey lit a cigarette. A blue haze of smoke hung in the air between them. 'She's not goin' on holiday.'

West could see the boy had something on his mind. 'You need a drink.' He got up and walked to the bar.

Davey followed him. 'You're suppose to be lookin' after her, Pauli.'

West went behind the jump and poured two brandies. 'What's that suppose to mean?'

Davey settled on a stool. 'She's screwing some Irish guy.'

For a second West froze. 'How do you know this?'

'I followed her. She went to this flat above an antique shop. Then he arrived. They was in there over an hour. Fucking whore!'

West was icily calm. 'What did he look like?'

'Big fucker. Walked like John Wayne.'

West knew this had to be Mahon.

Davey had no idea what he was setting in motion. 'I reckon she's runnin' off with him. Packed most of her stuff.'

West sipped his brandy. 'When is she leaving?'

'An airport car is picking her up at four.'

West smiled. 'I can't get over it. You could be Ray sitting there.'

Davey sensed something was on.

Thirty-Eight

Fran sat emotionally remote in the back of the airport car as it eased through the city. She thought she would be unhappy leaving, but she wasn't. There was a quiet regret but that was all. It was as though she had been living inside another woman and now she was free of her. In Spain she would be a stranger in a strange land, but at least she wouldn't have to lie to herself to escape herself. She glanced out of the window, then turned back to the driver. 'Is this the way to the airport?'

He talked to her over his shoulder. 'It's a longer way round but there's less traffic.'

Fran saw him dart a glance at the rear view mirror. She turned and looked through the back window at the car behind. Sunlight slanted off its windscreen. She couldn't quite make out the face of the driver but it looked like Seaman. A sudden apprehension took hold of her. She turned back. 'Where are we going?'

The driver accelerated.

'Where are you taking me?'

She glanced back again as they drove into a pool of shadow that cut out the sun's glare. It *was* Seaman, and with Soge beside him. Fran panicked and snatched the car door open.

The road was a tarmac blur.

The driver shouted. 'You'll kill yourself!'

Fran pulled the door closed, slid back in her seat and sat like stone.

As Mahon entered his flat, he saw it had been ripped apart. The dog was lying in a pool of blood underneath an upturned chair. Mahon ignored every instinct and moved into the room. He lifted the chair and bent down beside the dog. He saw it had been shot; it was only just alive, panting, it's tongue lolling from its mouth. He stroked it gently.

J.W. emerged from the bedroom, a silenced gun in his hand.

Mahon rose to face him.

He was badly marked from the beating, one eye was covered with a dressing, his head had been shaved where it had been stitched.

Mahon measured the distance between himself and the gun.

J.W. could read Mahon's thoughts. 'I could enjoy killing you.'

Soge appeared.

The telephone rang.

J.W. looked at it, then back to Mahon. 'That'll be for you.'

Mahon moved to the phone and lifted the receiver.

'John?' It was Fran.

'Yes.'

'Are you all right?'

Mahon could hear the anxiety in her voice. 'Yes.'

Her phone clicked dead.

Mahon slowly lowered the receiver and turned to J.W. 'Where is she?'

J.W. waved his gun to the door. 'Pauli's waiting.'

Soge moved behind Mahon and jabbed a gun in his back.

Mahon looked down at the dying dog, 'You can't leave him like that.'

J.W. turned his gun on the dog; the silenced shot sounded like a dropped egg breaking on a wooden floor.

Mahon sat between J.W. and Soge in the back of the car as it powered through the city, a gun pressed in his belly.

Thirty-Nine

West stood with Davey looking out at the city through a fourth-storey latticed window that stretched from ceiling to floor in an unconverted section of the warehouse. 'When we were kids your father and me used to say that one day we'd run this city.'

Davey was convinced his father would win the appeal. 'He'll be out soon.'

West turned to Davey. 'The appeal application has been knocked back.'

Davey couldn't believe it. 'What?'

'We've got his brief working on it.'

Davey punched one of the cracked panes of glass; it shattered. 'Fuck the brief! Fuck the appeal!' He sucked a bleeding knuckle. 'I'm gonna jump him out!'

Mahon climbed the seemingly endless stone stairway, J.W. and Soge two steps behind. He stopped and turned back to J.W. 'Is she here?'

Soge punched his gun painfully in Mahon's back. 'Shut your mouth and move!'

*   *   *

When Mahon entered he was surprised to see the boy who'd asked him the way to the restaurant. It didn't take him long to work out what had happened. It was Fran's son, he should have known; he had her face.

West turned from the window and looked at Mahon.

There was a dead weight of silence.

Mahon walked towards him. 'Where's Fran?'

The mention of his mother's name touched a nerve in Davey. He pulled his gun and punched it at Mahon. 'Let me kill him, Pauli!'

West was surprised that Davey was tooled. He moved from the window. 'Put that away.'

Davey glared at Mahon.

'Put it away!'

Davey spat in Mahon's face and lowered the gun.

Mahon raised a hand to wipe away the spittle as West crossed to him. 'Who are you?'

Mahon indicated J.W. with his head. 'You had your monkey check me out.'

J.W. cracked Mahon across the back of his head with his gun.

West moved closer. 'Tell me about Lynn.'

Blood seeped down the back of Mahon's head and dripped on to his jacket collar. He knew now that this was about more than Fran, but how much did Pauli West actually know? 'Who?'

'Major James Lynn?' West moved still closer, searching Mahon's face for any hint of recognition. 'Clever man. That shooting . . .'

Mahon heard an edge of doubt in West's voice; it was all he had to cling to. 'I don't know what you're talking about.'

West's face was only inches from Mahon's. 'Convince me.'

Mahon pointed at the still-healing scar on his neck. 'All I know about the shooting is this.'

West gestured to Mahon to follow him. They crossed the room and stood at the window looking down into a narrow street below where the airport car was parked. The driver stood beside it, smoking. 'She missed her flight,' West slipped an airline ticket from an inside pocket, 'but I've booked her another one.' He held it out to Mahon. 'First class.'

Mahon took the ticket, opened it and checked the date, the flight number and Fran's name.'

West took the ticket back. 'She thinks you're just a dealer.'

Mahon looked down again. He saw Fran being led to the car by Seaman.

West watched Mahon as he stared down at her. 'You're a dead man my friend. You've got nothing left to lose, but she has; her memories, they're all she's got.'

Mahon saw Fran look up at the window. Seaman grabbed her as she tried to run back into the warehouse.

'She was easy, wasn't she? Ray was a pig. She'd been unhappy for years. Then you turn up and sweet-talk her.'

Mahon watched as Seaman bundled Fran into the car and closed the door. She turned and strained to look up through the back window.

West turned the knife in Mahon's guilt. 'Fuck her for information. Orders from Lynn. You don't want her to know that, do you? You don't want her to go away knowing how you used her? Knowing what a piece of shit you really are?'

Mahon looked down at Fran. She was still looking up through the back window of the car, her face pale and lined like twisted linen. He turned back to West, overcome by the sheer force of his malice. 'What do you want?'

West tapped the ticket on his thumb. 'I want everything: Lynn's group, the set-up.'

Mahon wanted Fran safe. 'She goes now or you get nothing. She goes now and she rings me from the airport just before she boards her flight. Until then . . . nothing.'

West considered for a moment then passed the ticket to Soge. 'Give her your mobile. Tell her to ring J, she knows his number.' He turned back to Mahon, 'You try to lie – I'll break her heart.'

Soge left with the ticket.

Mahon turned back to the window and waited until he saw Soge at the car talking to Fran. He saw him hand her the ticket then his mobile. As the car drove away he saw Fran was still looking back. He remained staring out of the window, lost in the enigma of memory: the way she would run her fingers through her hair after they had made love, that secret smile that started in her eyes, the eloquence of her silence. Before he met Fran he had forgotten the power of human attachment, now all he felt was an overwhelming sadness that he would never see her again.

They waited in silence, strangely posed. West was the only one moving, pacing in a neat six step line, back and forth.

A mobile sang.

J.W. lifted it from his pocket and switched it on.

West stopped pacing and looked across at him.

J.W. nodded to confirm it was Fran.

West turned to Mahon. 'Lie. You're good at that.'

Mahon moved across to J.W. and took the mobile. 'Fran?'

'Pauli's promised he won't hurt you.'

Mahon looked at West, who was standing with his back to the window. 'We're sorting it out.'

'He promised me!'

Mahon tried to calm her. 'It's going to be okay, Fran.'

'Let me talk to Pauli.'

'Just get on the plane.'

'Let me talk to him.'

'You'll miss your flight.'

'I'm not leaving till I'm sure you're safe.'

'Get on the plane. Go where you're going. Let me know where you are and I'll be there.'

'When?'

'As soon as I can.' Mahon walked away a few steps so that his last words with Fran were private. He switched the mobile off and held it out. As J.W. went to take it, Mahon let it slip from his fingers. Instinctively J.W. went to catch it. Mahon grabbed and turned him as Soge went to shoot. Mahon felt his body take the impact of the shots. He released J.W. and he crumpled to the floor. In the confusion Mahon moved like an arrow towards West. Davey emptied his gun at Mahon: one shot hit him fatally in the back. Pain seared through his body, but by now he was on top of West who stood frozen, framed by the window. Mahon hurled himself at West and they went crashing back through it.

Splintered glass sprayed from the window. The two bodies fell through the darkness, their limbs entwined like lovers. They seemed to fall forever before hitting the ground. West lay dead, his limbs at odd angles.

Mahon lay dead a few feet away. A brightly-lit pleasure boat with a party on board went gliding past, faint music hung in the still night air.

Beyond the river the city squatted like a toad.